Suddenly Supernatural
SCHOOL SPIRIT

by
Elizabeth Cody Kimmel

LITTLE, BROWN AND COMPANY
Books for Young Readers

New York   Boston

Little, Brown and Company

Hachette Book Group USA
237 Park Avenue, New York, NY 10017
Visit our Web site at www.lb-kids.com

First Edition: June 2008

The characters and events portrayed in this book are
fictitious. Any similarity to real persons, living or dead,
is coincidental and not intended by the author.

Library of Congress Cataloging-in-Publication Data

Kimmel, Elizabeth Cody.
School spirit / by Elizabeth Cody Kimmel. — 1st ed.
p. cm. — (Suddenly supernatural)
Summary: Like her mother, a professional medium, Kat has been able to see
dead people since turning thirteen, and although they would prefer to be
normal, Kat and her best friend come to terms with their own talents while
helping free the spirit of a girl trapped at their middle school.
ISBN 978-0-316-06683-9 (alk. paper)
[1. Spiritualists—Fiction. 2. Mothers and daughters—Fiction.
3. Individuality—Fiction. 4. Self-acceptance—Fiction. 5. Musicians—
Fiction. 6. Popularity—Fiction. 7. Schools—Fiction.] I. Title.
PZ7.K56475Sch 2008
[Fic]—dc22   2007031542

10 9 8 7 6 5 4 3 2 1

RRD-C

Printed in the United States of America

The text was set in RuseX, and the display type is Oneleigh

~Suddenly~
Supernatural

SCHOOL | SPIRIT

Chapter 1

The undead are ruining my life. I blame my mother.

My mother is a medium. And I don't mean the kind that fits in between small and large. My mother is your basic incense-burning, Indian-skirt-wearing vegetarian who happens to see and interact with dead people. You cannot imagine the humiliation this causes me, being the junior high newbie that I am. Because here's the thing — like my uncle Steve, who thinks it's okay to ask me all about the boys in my class, the dead have *major* boundary issues. When the dead are earthbound and confused and channeling their anger into ordinary household objects, they're not really interested in confining their activities to the attention of the person summoning them. No, all those delightful supernatural activities that happen in movies — abrupt temperature changes, earsplitting sounds, and other spirit-induced phenomena — affect everyone unfortunate enough to be living in the house. Namely, *me.*

I could put my foot down, I guess. I could tell my mother she is ruining my life, scarring me emotionally during my crucial early adolescent years, and virtually guaranteeing that I have years of therapy ahead of me. I could tell her those things. I could demand that she put aside who she is for the next five or ten years, get a little MTV-literate, read an issue of *Cosmo* every now and then, and basically get with the decade. I could ask her to leave the dead alone. To just ignore their pleas. And knowing her, she'd probably try. But that's the problem. Knowing her.

This is the same mother who proclaims a Bossing Day once a year, when I get to be in charge and ask for ice-cream sundaes for breakfast. I'm allowed to take control of the remote, go shopping for no reason, or watch the latest Orlando Bloom movie twice in the actual movie theater, with buttered popcorn *and* candy. This is the same mother who knows the difference between a bad day and a devastating day, who knows exactly how to rub my feet to make the rest of me feel better, who knows the perfect temperature for a bubble bath. The same mother who knows when *not* to ask how I am. The same mother who let me take a mental health day and skip school in second grade after a note I intended for one girl ended up in the hands of the boy it was written about.

You see my problem. This is not a mother who *should* really change. She's kind of great the way she is. It's the world of junior high that needs to change. But the last time I looked out the window, it was the same old world, both at school and outside of it. And in the same old world, having a mother who is an Olympic-class magnet for supernatural activity is uncool. And being uncool can ruin a person's life, especially when that someone doesn't happen to be all that cool to begin with. Don't get me wrong. I'm not saying it's more important for me to be cool than to support my mom. It's just that I kind of want both.

Last month, my teacher assigned Shoshanna Longbarrow as my research partner for our Hoover Dam social studies project. I'd been living in Medford for more than a year, and Shoshanna had never so much as acknowledged me with a "Hey." Still, I knew that she was the Girl to Know. A seat at her lunch table was the Holy Grail of middle-school life. I had never been granted one. So you can imagine my surprise when Shoshanna Longbarrow addressed me in person the same day we were assigned to work together. And it was like we'd been casually chatting for years.

"So I hear you're, like, this total straight A student or something. I guess you've pretty much got this Hoover Dam thing all figured out?" she asked.

And I knew, because we were the only two people in the room and only my mother talks to people who aren't there, that Shoshanna Longbarrow was talking to *me.*

"I guess," I said.

I affected a neutral look while my mind worked furiously. I did have a rap as a good student. I'd done my best to disguise the extent of my good grades, because nobody wants to hang out with a 4.0 girl, but apparently the word had gotten out anyway. And it was no secret that Shoshanna frequently pronounced good grades useless, probably because she got so few of them herself. Shoshanna definitely had the immaculately groomed look of a girl who needed big-time help with her social studies project research. I figured that maybe this was the break I needed to finally get in good with Shoshanna.

"Whatevs," Shoshanna said, shrugging. And like the announcer on a TV commercial, a voice in my head screamed, "ACT NOW! DON'T DELAY! LIMITED SUPPLIES AVAILABLE! OPERATORS STANDING BY!"

"I can show you what I've got so far so you don't have to do the same work again," I said.

Shoshanna stuck her hand out, palm down. If she'd been one of my mother's friends, I would have guessed she was preparing for a tarot card reading, or harnessing the energy of Mother Earth. Was this some kind of elite hand signal?

"Your address," Shoshanna commanded. "Write it down."

I obeyed, temporarily tattooing the back of her hand with my street digits.

"I'll be there right after school," Shoshanna told me.

And that is how, after months of being invisible, last May I suddenly found Shoshanna Longbarrow at my house.

Chapter 2

Obviously, this wasn't the way I would have planned our first get-together. It was a teacher-enforced gathering, after all. And the setting could have been better. Even on the best of days, my house, one of those creaky old Victorian things, was kind of like the Museum of Lost Hippie Artifacts. It was in need of a paint job, smelled of something between incense and old books, and was decorated in the Tibetan knickknack style. I was also more than a little nervous about Shoshanna running into my mother. To be honest, I was afraid my mother might be wearing something strange, like her harem pants. I've actually worn the harem pants, and they're unbelievably comfortable with their elastic waistband and balloon legs that button at the bottom, but they're not the kind of thing you want your mother wearing when you bring a popular girl home.

The door at the end of the hall was closed, which probably meant she was in a session. I *thought* this was a good thing.

I'd led Shoshanna into our "living room," which in our house is more an ironic designation than an actual room description. Like I said before, the dead have serious boundary issues, such as occasionally wandering out of the room my mother used for medium sessions to hang out in the living room, despite their not being living. Sadly, this was to be one of those days.

Shoshanna, after some obvious hesitation, had taken a seat on the overstuffed couch that was covered by a handwoven and half-disintegrated Tibetan rug. I offered her a plate of assorted cookies that my mother had left for my snack. Shoshanna grabbed two, a sugar cookie and a peanut butter cookie with a Hershey's Kiss pressed onto the top. As she bit into the sugar cookie, her eyes rolled up slightly and she made a little cooing sound of happiness. My mother's cookies had pretty much the same effect on everyone.

"My mother made them," I explained.

Shoshanna flapped one hand in the air to indicate her approval of this fact. When she finished chewing, she said, "You are *so* lucky. My mother would, like, *never* bake. I mean, even if she could, which she can't, she would never have cookies in the house.

Counting calories is, like, her religion. If I get a rice cake and a some celery sticks after school I consider it a good day."

"That's nuts," I said. "Look at you. There's not an ounce of fat on you."

Shoshanna rewarded me with a wide smile, so I went in for a little more small talk.

"So, Mrs. Logan in French, what does she have, like, three outfits, total?"

Shoshanna's face lit up at the introduction of faculty gossip. "I know!" she exclaimed, her mouth still partly full of cookie. I took her enthusiasm as a good sign and went with it.

"She's got the tan pantsuit. And she's got the black polka-dotted skirt with the shirt that has the matching print in the reversed pattern. And then she's got the navy —"

"Blue blazer with ruffles and matching pants!" Shoshanna interrupted. "Exactly!

And she never wears anything else! Just one of those three!"

"Maybe we could give her a new outfit!" I said, eagerly. "You know, like, anonymously."

"Yeah, right?" Shoshanna said, preparing to start in on the second cookie. "Like basic black Donna Karan pants with a teal sweater set. We could leave a bag with her name on it in the faculty lounge."

Before I could begin expanding on the style and color scheme of this hypothetical charity outfit, the temperature in the room dropped a good fifteen or twenty degrees. I pretended not to notice.

"It just got, like, super *FREEZING* in here!" Shoshanna said, pausing with the cookie halfway to her mouth.

I glanced up and tried to put on a look of genuine surprise.

"Did it?" I asked. My breath hung in a frozen cloud in front of my face like an exclamation point. I knew right then that my mother was definitely conducting a session in her room down the hall. Apparently, a successful one. And whoever it was she was trying to contact had just arrived, bringing a cold front of arctic proportions with them.

"It's these old houses," I added quickly. "The heat is, like, impossible to regulate in the winter."

"But it's April!"

I dismissed this unarguable fact by shaking my head.

"The furnace will kick back on in a minute," I said. "So anyway, I've already printed out eight pages of historical research on the Hoover Dam, and I've got a copy of a map of the Colorado River that charts the areas receiving irrigation or electrical power. We might as well just include all this in our joint research presentation. The work's already done, after all."

Shoshanna stared at me, confused. My tactic of distracting her from the icy room by dangling already completed research for which she could get class credit seemed to be working. She looked at my notes with interest, but the map seemed to totally flummox her. I didn't point out that she was looking at it upside down. Frankly, I'm guessing that before getting to my house today, Shoshanna had thought the Hoover Dam was some kind of vacuum cleaner attachment. I pushed my notebook toward her.

"These are notes I made from a PBS special I rented from the library," I said. "Copy them if you want." I couldn't believe I had just said that. I *hated* copiers! Was all this worth it to get Shoshanna to like me?

I might have had a chance to work through this moral struggle if the house hadn't erupted at that moment with the sound of bagpipes blaring a random mixture of Scottish folk tunes and squawks. And a smell washed over the room at the same time. Something like hay, and mud, and thistle flower. Shoshanna looked deeply alarmed by the sound and the smell. I thought fast, grasping for an explanation.

"Sorry," I said, rolling my eyes. "That noise is the furnace. And the boiler. They make that noise when they switch on at the same time."

Shoshanna continued to look rattled, and she still had not taken a bite of the second cookie. This was a bad sign. Shoshanna was obviously spooked. I needed to redirect her attention again. I'd have to appeal to her lazy research attitude.

"So did you want to copy these notes, or would you prefer to watch the three-hour PBS thing and make your own notes?"

I slid my notes closer to Shoshanna. That's when the howling started. A series of yelps, keens, and yowls reverberated throughout the house. Shoshanna's jaw dropped.

"That's just my, uh, Aunt Ellen. She's visiting. She's, like, this actress, actually." Shoshanna stared, and I kept blabbering.

". . . a Method actress, actually, that's what they call it, I think, and she does this vocal warm-up thing based on an ancient, um, Chinese dialect —"

It was too late. Whether or not she knew I didn't actually have an Aunt Ellen in the house, she seemed to suspect there was something . . . wrong going on.

"There's something totally weird about this house," Shoshanna said.

"What do you —"

"One minute it's normal, the next minute it's freezing. Then there's this horrible squawking, then some chick starts howling. Something isn't right here. Just because I'm not an honor roll nerd doesn't mean I'm stupid. I've felt creeped out since the moment I walked through your front door. It's, like . . . I don't know. Your house is possessed, or whatever. And if you can pretend there's nothing going on, you must be some majorly warped kind of freak."

Okay. This was not how I'd hoped my visit with Shoshanna was going to go. My first one-on-one visit with her was obviously going to be my last. I would never be welcome at her lunch table now. Then I had an even worse thought. It was bad enough that Shoshanna had experienced what she had in my house. What if she went to school and told other people about it? What if the entire school knew by tomorrow?

Destination: Warped Freakville. Population: Me.

Then I said something I probably shouldn't have.

"Think what you want to think, Shoshanna. But if you're not stupid, like you say, you won't go telling everyone at school about it. Because, you know, they'll just think that *you're* the one who's nuts. I mean, come on. A house that's possessed? Do you actually believe in that stuff? They'll laugh at you."

Shoshanna narrowed her eyes meanly at me, and I knew I'd crossed a line. Nobody threatened Shoshanna. Even I knew that.

"Brooklyn won't," she said, adding a sly smile. "And Brooklyn *hates* freaks."

That was when I saw the lamp on the table behind her rise several feet in the air, tilt thirty degrees to the left, and execute a graceful midair pirouette before landing daintily where it had been. Things were just going from bad to nightmare. I had to get Shoshanna out of my house before anything worse happened, like ectoplasm oozing out of the walls, or luminescent spirit orbs hovering.

"Fine, then, just go!" I said.

Shoshanna, half into her jacket and already on edge, leaped to her feet.

"Oh, trust me, I am," she said.

"So, have fun doing all this research yourself!" I yelled as she headed for the door. "Because this isn't exactly making me want to help you out!"

"Don't flatter yourself. I have other ways to get it done," Shoshanna snapped. She turned to glare at me just as the bagpipes started up again. If she had been planning on saying anything else, she changed her mind and hightailed it out the front door.

It was out of my hands now. Shoshanna had experienced something supernatural in my house, and she knew it. She'd either use the information to make my life miserable, or she wouldn't. The situation was no longer in my control.

When my mom came out of her session room about an hour later, I heard her saying good-bye to a woman I didn't get a look at. Then she came into the living room and found me curled up on the overstuffed couch.

"Did I hear voices?" she asked.

"You've been hearing voices since you were thirteen years old, Mom," I said, rolling my eyes.

She smiled. She *was* wearing the harem pants. With a big, wool sweater held closed by an enormous diaper pin. The right designer could probably charge a thousand dollars for this look, popularized by Mary Kate Olsen as Dumpster chic.

"I thought you might have had company," she said. "I was worried my session might get too loud or something. This woman was looking for an ancestor who turned out to have been a pipe major for the Scottish Black Watch Regiment at the Battle of Waterloo."

That explained the squawking noises. Rather than try to make up a story minimizing Shoshanna's hasty departure, I just gave my mother a smile.

"Sounds like a successful session!" I exclaimed.

She smiled and put her arm around me, successfully distracted.

You see, this is my problem. I haven't been able to tell my mother the simple truth, that the spirits people ask her to summon, or the spirits that simply show up looking for help, sometimes make it almost impossible for me to have a normal seventh-grade existence. Forget about Shoshanna for a minute. I don't see how *anybody* would want to hang out with me for more than a few weeks. Stuff happens all the time. Over the summer we were in the meat section of the Foodtown, and two frozen Cornish game hens levitated themselves into my mother's shopping cart. She said the floating poultry was meant to be an innocent hello from a spirit who enjoyed pulling harmless pranks, but all I cared about was that my English teacher, Mr. Lamar, was a few feet down the aisle buying bologna and almost saw the whole thing. Then there was the time she came to school to pick me up early for a doctor's appointment, and as she walked me down the hallway the lights of every classroom she passed, including my own, flickered off. Fortunately, nobody noticed the lights going out with her. But one day, somebody will see her when something freaky is happening, and they'll put two and two together. It's just a matter of time.

And it gets even more complicated. The way she sees these spirits and everything. Because after I turned thirteen a few months ago, I started to see them, too.

And that's so not cool.

Chapter 3

I had noticed the girl in the school halls before. She'd be hard to miss. She was a tiny redheaded girl, maybe ninety pounds soaking wet, and every time I caught sight of her she was dragging this enormous cello case. It looked really ridiculous. Have you ever seen an ant find a big crumb of cake that's, like, three times its size and then haul it back to the anthill? That's what this girl looked like lugging her giant cello around. She had showed up as a new student in school in March, when the third trimester began.

I kind of felt a kinship with her, since I'd been new the year before. Being the new girl in sixth grade can be outdone in terms of sheer horror only by being the new girl in seventh grade. Not to mention the trauma of showing up more than halfway through the year, when everybody already has their friends and the pecking order is more or less carved in stone. The girl had an uphill battle at school, and that made me want to help her. But the cello thing was sort of bizarre. Certain people made a point of snickering when she pulled the massive instrument down the hall. I was lonely, but I wasn't sure I wanted to be known as the One Who Hangs Out with Cello Girl.

But as it turns out, I wasn't really given a choice. The day after my Shoshanna disaster, I was facing that daily scholastic experience that haunts the dreams of every new kid in the history of school: walking into the cafeteria with my lunch tray and looking for a seat. I was relieved to learn that Shoshanna herself was not in school that day, postponing my fear that she would broadcast the news of my bizarre home situation to the four corners of the earth. But even knowing Shoshanna wasn't there, my stomach still tightened as I looked around for a table. I'm sure it's the same at all schools, the basic rundown being that there's a brain table, a jock table, a princess/cheerleader table, a hip-hop table, a goth table, and a computer geek table. Those are all off limits to outsiders. There is no table for Girls Whose Moms Chat with the Dearly Departed, and I'd like to keep it that way. Then there are some midlist spillover tables, for people who don't really fit into a specific group but aren't officially outcasts. If you get to lunch too late and there aren't any midlist

spillover seats left, you have to choose between outcast and starvation. Starvation,
clearly, being the superior choice.

That's how I ended up sitting with Cello
Girl. I was late getting to lunch, and she had
taken a spot at the last available midlist table. She was actually taking up two spots,
because her cello case was leaning on the
chair next to her, and no one else was at the
table. So it was Cello Girl or starvation, and
I'd skipped breakfast that morning. I sat
down across the table from her and hoped
she might think I was hearing impaired and
not bother trying any chitchat.

"I'm Jac," she said. "No *k*. J-A-C. Short
for Jacqueline, which is too tall a name for
me, and I can't stand Jackie, because it's
infantalizing."

"I'm Kat," I replied. "With a *K*." Jac
nodded, like the name was a good fit

for my height. She didn't explain what infantalizing meant. It sounded vaguely vampire-oriented.

"Nice earrings," she said.

That threw me slightly, because the earrings in question were tiny silver skeletons, with real moving arms and legs, that my mom had brought me after she went to the Day of the Dead festival in Mexico. Not exactly regulation accessories for your normal Medford non-goth seventh-grader. But it made my mom so happy when I wore them, I put them on every now and again just to see her smile. Today, I'd forgotten to take them off before getting to school.

"Thanks," I said. "My mom gave them to me."

"She must be cool," Jac said.

Oh, if only she knew what passed for "cool" around my house! But I couldn't help feeling a little pleased at the compliment. And surprised, given Jac was wearing a turtleneck and an L.L.Bean sweater. She didn't look like the type to appreciate functional human skeleton earrings.

I watched her eat for a moment. She had pale ivory skin and fine, delicate features. She looked like a pixie. I felt an urge to push her hair away from her face to see if her ears were pointed.

"So you just moved here?" I asked, stabbing at my milk carton with a straw.

"Yeah, from Ithaca," she replied. Jac had an easy way about her. I sensed she was one of those unusual people who felt basically comfortable in her own skin.

"Did your mom or dad come for a job or something?" I asked. Usually when a kid moved to or from Medford, it was either because of their parents' work or one of those divorce things, because we're a pretty out-of-the-way place with not much around except for a big computer company. Some people said Medford put the "up" in upstate New York. Lucky us.

"We came for a cello teacher, actually," replied Jac. "A retired cello virtuoso who used to be pretty famous lives in Medford. Somewhat of a recluse, but she teaches a few students. I go two, sometimes three days a week after school, so I have to bring my cello with me. Plus, I'm supposed to rehearse every day in the music room before school starts."

"Wow," I said. "You must be good."

Jac shrugged.

"It's just what I do," she said, somewhat cryptically.

We ate in silence for a while, but it was a friendly silence, like these two auburn-haired seventh-grade girls I always saw who'd been best friends forever since kindergarten and ate lunch at one of the midlist spillover tables each day, sharing every single item of food in their lunch boxes. Eventually a few kids who couldn't find anywhere else to go sat at our table, but they talked among themselves at their end, and Jac and I ignored them.

After a while, Jac looked up at the clock by the exit.

"Uh-oh. I've got to move," she said.

"There's ten minutes left before next period," I pointed out.

"Gotta take care of the old ball and chain," she replied.

"Ball and chain?"

Jac patted her cello case affectionately.

"Takes me a little longer to get around than regular people."

And that was pretty much it. Jac dragged her cello out of the cafeteria, somehow managing not to hit anyone on the way out, and she was gone. But over the next few days, during which Shoshanna continued to be absent (I heard something about her grandmother having died), the situation kept repeating itself. Jac and I would end up sitting together with her ball and chain at one of the midlist tables. By the end of the week, I realized I was actually looking for her in the lunchroom. Looking forward to seeing her. And she always saved my seat. We started to trade the little life histories you go into when you're getting to know someone. Just the basic stuff. Her dad worked as a computer genius for a local corporation. My dad split five years ago. She'd once had a lab-beagle mix named Darwin, but they had to give it away when her mother developed allergies.

We had no pets, in spite of my desperate yearning for a puppy. We were both only children. That kind of thing.

And I just realized, after a while, I had a friend. I'd been pretty much invisible at school for more than a year, and now I had a friend. To say it felt good was an understatement. It made me understand how those spirits who found my mom must feel. They hung around for years, decades, even centuries, being invisible to everyone around them. Then one day my mother *saw* them. And they were so happy just to be seen, she immediately became their new best friend.

Jac saw me. And I liked it.

When I got home from school on Friday, my mom was sitting at the kitchen table, reading a letter by candlelight. We *can* afford electricity, if just barely. Between the occasional checks she got from her family in the mail and what she earned giving sessions, we got by well enough to keep the place lit and heated. But my mom preferred doing things by candlelight. Beeswax candles. She said they emitted negatively charged ions into the room that cleared mental clutter away and made the air feel rich, like when a big thunderstorm was about to roll in. After much personal experience with the candles, I kind of agreed — the candles did something. Plus, with her long, baby-fine blond hair and the faded Peruvian wrap draped over her shoulders, my mother looked like a flower child in the flickering light. I liked it. It was a little like being at summer camp in your own kitchen. I pulled up a chair.

"Hey, sweetie," she said, folding her letter and smiling at me.

"Hey," I said, smiling back. "Whaddya got there? Jury duty summons? Fan mail?"

"Someone asking for help," she said, unfolding the paper. "She can't or won't come by in person."

"Again? I don't get it. If someone believes in your gift enough to ask for your help, why would they have a problem showing up in person?"

I couldn't help but be irritated. It bothered me how sometimes the same people my mother helped would look the other way when they ran into her at Foodtown. Like they were embarrassed to know her. My mother just shrugged.

"People are complicated, Kat," she said. "There are plenty of reasons people might feel conflicted about trying to reach a loved one who has passed over. If they're coming to me for help, they're probably in pain. They don't need to be judged on top of everything else."

It was when my mother said things along those lines that I felt most deeply that I would never be as strong, or as good, or as kind as she was, no matter how hard I tried. Where she saw someone in pain, I just saw someone being rude.

"I know I shouldn't judge them. I just feel like people should be polite to you," I said quietly. "People ought to show you respect."

She smiled. "I tell you, kiddo. I wouldn't turn down a little respect if it came my way."

"I respect you," I said.

She smiled again. "I know you do, sweetie."

I was curious to see the letter but knew better than to ask. Every once in a while my mother would share the story of the people she was working with, or more rarely let me read the letters people wrote to her. Usually they got right to the point, something along the lines of:

Dear Medium Lady,

How are you? I am fine. Please summon my dead Aunt Tootie and ask her where the key to the silver chest is. Hope all is well with the underworld.

Sincerely,
Fake Name

But more often people requested complete discretion on my mother's part, which basically meant don't tell *anyone* I'm asking you to help me, and we will of course pretend we don't know each other if we ever come face-to-face in public, because this is really nothing more than a simple business arrangement.

Don't ask, don't tell.

My mother stared at the letter for a moment, a slight frown on her forehead.

"Are you getting anything?" I asked.

She closed her eyes for a moment, then shook her head.

"Nothing. Not a thing. But I'll hear what's meant to be heard when the time is right. Do you have much homework?"

I shook my head.

"There might be some *Star Trek* reruns on the Sci-Fi channel."

I shook my head again.

"Want to order in some Chinese food?"

"I'm not sure I'm in the mood for Chinese," I said. But I could tell she wanted to do something together, so I made a counteroffer.

"We could walk down to the river," I said.

"Yeah, great!" she said. "We could go by the bakery and get some of that organic hot cider and cinnamon doughnuts from the Whole Foods market on the way back."

My mouth watered. As usual, I didn't really know what I wanted until I heard my mother say it. I shrugged into my coat as she blew out the candle.

"Got any news for me?" she asked as we walked down the creaky front hall to the door.

"Actually, I think I've kind of made a friend at school," I said.

She paused with her hand on the door-knob to look at me. Her face was so eager and optimistic I vowed that if Jac didn't end up wanting to hang out with me, I'd just invent a friend so she'd stay this happy.

"Oh, Kat, that's so great. Tell me about her."

"Well," I began as we walked out of the house, "she does kind of come with some baggage."

It was when we were down near the river, after finishing our cider and doughnuts, that it happened. You see, I'm not personally experienced in these things yet. I barely know what's even happening half the time. And the light was fading, and I was distracted and thrilled and terrified by how happy the mention of Jac had made my mother. So, we were strolling kind of slowly, and as I walked past an elderly gentleman who was wearing a long black coat and an ancient-looking hat, I veered too close and accidentally brushed his arm as I passed him. And just as a reflex, I said, "Excuse me."

My mom froze next to me, and in a split second I realized what I'd done. I'd been too absorbed in our conversation to appreciate the flatness of the man, the air of electricity buzzing around him. The sense of other-dimensionality.

The man I'd just spoken to was not alive.

My mother was looking intensely into my eyes. She put her hands on my shoulders.

"Kat," she said, quietly. "What did you just say?"

Chapter 4

Staring into my mother's green-gold eyes, I was gripped by the impulse to tell her all of it, what little there was. That it had begun three days after my most recent birthday, when two little girls dressed for a costume party had caught my attention walking on the sidewalk by our house. That I'd been watching them for almost a minute when I realized no one else was smiling at them as I was, that others on the sidewalk did not even bother to get out of the girls' way as they strolled. And that in spite of the blazing late summer sun, their little figures cast no shadows. That the very microsecond I had realized I was seeing spirits, one of them turned and fixed me with an intent, pleading look, and I turned and ran away like a frightened deer. And that there were two other times since then I'd seen the dead walking. Or, counting today, three. I could have told her right then, plain and simple.

Instead, I lied.

"I said excuse me," I told my mother, shifting my gaze a fraction to the side of her face. "I cranked out a nice cidery burp. You can't tell me you didn't hear it!"

She hesitated for just a tiny moment, but I felt it. There was something she had decided not to say. She felt like my twin, sometimes, the way I could pick things like that up.

"That was you?" she asked, tugging

playfully on my scarf. "I thought there was a barge coming up the river, blaring the foghorn."

"Oh, I'm just getting started," I said. "Wait till after dinner — I'll sound like a whole fleet of barges."

She chuckled, and linked her arm through mine.

We had reached the end of the paved river promenade, and in tandem we turned around and began walking back. I saw, to my relief, that the man in the dark coat had disappeared. He was probably not one of those spirits seeking communication. More likely just a spirit unwilling to give up his evening stroll, even a half century or so after his legs stopped working for good. Harmless.

I had shamed myself into silence with my lie. To make cheerful chatter now would just seem like more lies. As usual, my mother seemed to sense I needed her to make most of the conversation on the way home.

"Oh, Kat, I saw the funniest thing at the Laundromat today. There was this really young guy doing his laundry, and it looked like he'd never done it himself before. And he'd tossed in this tie-dyed orange shirt with a bunch of white stuff, and when he pulled the load out it had all turned orange. . . . The *look* on this guy's face!" I listened, smiling and nodding and laughing when I was meant to, but all I could really think about was what a small, mean thing I'd done. Lying to her. Just when I thought I couldn't possibly feel any worse, she added something.

"The thing is, Kat, I saw something else in the Laundromat, and I've been thinking about it all day. I know how badly you've been wanting a dog."

I literally froze, my heart pounding.

A dog? I wanted one so badly the mere thought of it made me cry, but puppies were expensive and hard to take care of and weren't inclined to keep quiet during a session and . . .

"Now don't get *too* excited — it isn't a puppy," she said quickly, reading my mind, as usual. "It's a grown dog. Five years old. A German shepherd. The flyer says the family is moving overseas, and they're looking for a loving home for him."

I didn't say anything, because I didn't trust myself to speak. German shepherd was one of my favorite breeds. I held my breath and waited for my mother to continue.

"I did give them a call," my mother said. "And they live near the Laundromat, so I swung by to have a look at him. Name is Max. He's a beauty, I have to say. Intelligent, gentle. And comfortable around spirits, at least the two who live in his house. The family doesn't know, obviously, that they're sharing the house with two old ladies who died in the nineteen forties, but Max gets along with them just fine. They were quite nice to me, too. I don't know, what do you think?"

I nodded so vigorously one of my earrings swung back and attached itself to my hair. My mother had a smile playing about her mouth, a smile that kept growing as she watched me.

"Yeah? Should we?"

"Yes!" I shouted. "Yes, yes, yes!" And I threw my arms around her and danced her back and forth along the sidewalk. "When can we bring Max home?"

I loved her so much in that moment I can hardly describe it. I was almost happy enough to blurt out the truth about how I'd started seeing spirits. But I couldn't. That would make it real, and I didn't want it to be real. I wasn't like my mother. I didn't have her strength, her kindness. I didn't think I had what it took to be a practicing medium.

Spirits are like babies. They scream and howl when they need something, and they'll go right on doing it until you fix their problem. And, again like babies, spirits are often unable to tell you what's wrong, or what they need. You can't just turn them off if you're tired or need a break from helping them. And being a medium is a constant reminder of the pain possible in life. You have to deal with all those rude, complicated people who want to hire you but ignore you in the supermarket. I just didn't know if I could ever face all that, a lifetime of service and responsibility, the way she had. Plus, I didn't like babies of any variety. Much better to start with a grown dog.

So, like a celebrity stepping onto the red carpet as the paparazzi snapped pictures, I walked along the river smiling and talking about Max, pretending for all the world that neither one of us knew I was hiding something.

We brought him home that night. My mother and I both believe that dogs have souls, and Max was an old soul indeed. His owners, an older childless couple, didn't want to drag out the good-byes any longer than they had to, so after they handed us a big pillow that Max liked to sleep on, a leash, and a bag of his favorite food, we were on our way.

It never ceases to amaze me how life can change all of a sudden. Three hours before I didn't have a dog. Then I was walking the world's most beautiful German shepherd back toward our house, my mother lugging his bed alongside us. When your mother works as a medium, there isn't too much spare cash to throw around on luxury items. But at that moment, approaching our house with Max in the lead, I felt like the most indulged kid in town.

When we got to our front walk, Max turned and pulled the leash to the right as he started up the steps.

"Now how did he know that?" my mother asked.

"Maybe he has a good nose," I said, following Max as he approached the door. When he reached the welcome mat, he sat down and turned to watch my mother.

"He's waiting for you to unlock it," I said.

It certainly seemed like that was exactly what Max was doing.

I held the dog bed while Mom got the door open. I dropped the leash and let Max go into the house under his own steam. I wanted him to be able to explore at will, so that he would feel comfortable and know that the house was his, too.

"So we'll set up his bowls in the kitchen, and what do you think about the bed, Kat? I thought it might go well in the living room under that corner window. You know, the one that gets the sun every day. And who knows — maybe Max will want to sleep on the foot of your bed at night?"

"Can he? I would *love* that!"

Part of my having a dog fantasy was that my dog would curl up at my feet each night, and we would snore blissfully together. Max was a big dog, granted, but I definitely wanted him with me at night.

"Let's just see where he goes at bedtime,"

my mom said. "He seems to know what he wants."

"It's like he already understands that he's moving in with us," I said.

My mother laughed.

"To say the least," she said. "Okay, let's bring this pillow into the living room and see how it fits under that window."

We both walked into the living room at the same time and froze just inside the doorway.

Max was lying in the corner under the window, in the exact place the sun would be coming in during the daytime.

"Well," my mother said with a laugh, "we were right. This dog definitely knows what he wants. And he seems to know what we want, too."

"Maybe he's psychic," I said. I'm not even sure it was a joke.

Much later that night, when I was curled up in bed with a novel, Max padded quietly into my room, jumped up on my bed, and curled his large, beautiful body into a tight circle — on top of my feet. Close enough.

There were two things that ultimately cemented my friendship with Jac. The first was the cafeteria incident, and the second was the attack of the Satellite Girl. For the record, a Satellite Girl is any of a number of ten or eleven girls who constantly revolve around the celestial entity known as Shoshanna Longbarrow. Their number and orbital paths occasionally change, but at any given hour of the day Shoshanna is generally being orbited by at least two Satellite Girls.

Jac and I were sitting together eating lunch when I saw a clipboard-wielding

Shoshanna bearing down on me. My heart immediately sank. Though I wasn't happy about anybody's grandmother dying, I had enjoyed having Shoshanna absent from school. But she'd returned to school last week, and now she was heading toward me at warp speed. I needed no psychic ability to know what was coming. Shoshanna was about to press me into service in the name of one of her monstrously evil organizations — in this instance, the Dance Decoration Committee. It was the very last thing I wanted to be involved in. But it had been two weeks since the disastrous outbreak of supernatural activity in my house during Shoshanna's visit, and though her friend Brooklyn had been doing a great bit of smirking in my direction, no one had said a thing to me about it. Shoshanna lost interest in gossip that she deemed too "yesterday," so maybe she'd decided not to spread the word beyond Brooklyn. Though I no longer entertained any possibility that Shoshanna and I would one day be best buds, I was relieved not to be a public laughingstock and wanted to avoid giving Shoshanna any further reason to hate me.

Because she was popular, Shoshanna had acquired a great deal of power, and because she was powerful she had acquired even more popularity. It was the old chicken-and-egg conundrum adapted to the junior high school pecking order. As head of the Dance Decoration Committee, Shoshanna was in charge of both choosing the theme and executing the decor for school dances. The choosing part she did herself, but the execution was usually delegated (by force) to others.

Shoshanna arrived at our table and stood importantly, clicking her ballpoint pen to indicate her orders were forthcoming.

"Kat," she stated, "I'm going to need some help with the prep for next Saturday's dance. As you know, the theme for the dance is world gems. I need construction paper cutouts of diamonds, rubies, emeralds, and sapphires, and an assortment of star and moon shapes for the sky. About a hundred and fifty of each. The materials are all in the art room. If you could go ahead and stay after school today and get that done, that would be fab."

Shoshanna always issued her orders this way. She'd "like you to go ahead and do this," as if it was something you'd seriously been considering doing all day anyway. And the little addendum, "That would be fab," was equally meaningless. I had been chosen and given my instructions. Resistance was futile. People always did what Shoshanna told them to, because she could and would do everything in her power to make the lives of those who defied her miserable. And as I've said, her power was considerable. Mine, to say the least, was not.

I was opening my mouth to unhappily agree that it would indeed be fab for me to spend three hours of my free time cutting out jewels and astronomical shapes from construction paper when Jac interrupted.

"She can't."

Shoshanna stared at Jac, temporarily at a loss for words. She looked thoroughly confused, the way she had the day we'd begun discussing the Hoover Dam.

"Excuse me?" Shoshanna said finally, with exquisite politeness.

"Kat can't help you out today. We're working on a bio project together in the library."

Shoshanna let out a small laugh of astonishment, glancing around to see if anyone else was witnessing this moment of magnificent comedy.

"Well," she began, the laugh still in her voice, "that's great, but I really do need my gems and stars and moons. You're the new girl, aren't you? Maybe you didn't realize, but I'm the head of the DDC, the Dance Decoration Committee. So I'm afraid Kat is going to need to go ahead and help me out today."

"She can't," Jac said firmly. "She's coming to the library with me. You'll just need to *go ahead* and ask someone else."

Shoshanna was so completely unaccustomed to hearing anyone say the word *can't*, that she simply stood there, her mouth hanging open.

"You ready, Kat?" Jac said, standing up. "Give me a hand with the ball and chain, won't you?"

I hesitated for one moment. Here I had just been feeling fortunate that Shoshanna hadn't informed most of her minions about the episode at my house. If I committed this new act of rebellion, she might decide to tell everyone just to get me back, even if the news was extremely "yesterday." But the reality was that Shoshanna would probably always have something on me, and she certainly would never be my friend. Jac *was* my friend. The decision was made. I took one end of Jac's cello case, though I knew she was perfectly capable of dragging it out of the cafeteria without any help, and we left Shoshanna Longbarrow standing alone by the now empty midlist spillover table.

Chapter 5

As we walked through the double doors leading to the hallway, I felt a small sense of exhilaration. I also felt a healthy dose of impending doom.

"We're working on the bio project together?" I asked.

"It's not like we don't need to get it done," Jac replied. "I don't have a cello lesson today — we can start it right after last bell. Anyway, you needed some intervention. A person doesn't need to be a genius to see you didn't want to do that girl's tracing and cutting for her."

"Thanks for the assist, Jac, but I'm not sure it was such a good idea," I said.

Jac turned and peered at me, narrowing her green eyes.

"Meaning you were aching inside to spend hours cutting out all the shapes in Lucky Stars cereal for some tiara girl who doesn't usually give you the time of day, to decorate a dance I'm betting that you have no intention of attending?"

I wasn't quite ready to tell Jac that I felt cautious about how I treated Shoshanna because a nineteenth-century Scottish bagpiper had frightened her at my house, since that would involve explaining what a roaming spirit was doing stopping off in my living room in the first place. Best to let it go.

"Well, when you put it that way . . ." I said, smiling. "But seriously, Jac. Take it from me. I was here all last year. I saw what happened to people who rubbed Shoshanna the wrong way. It's easier to just smile and nod when she volunteers you for something than to become the center of one of her dramas."

"You can't be serious," Jac said. "Those girls, Shoshanna and her little worshippers, you can't possibly stand there with a straight face and tell me their approval is important to you."

I cringed inwardly at the memory of how, not too long ago, Shoshanna's approval had actually been *quite* important to me. But Jac wasn't asking about not too long ago, she was asking about now. And I had Jac now.

"Of course not," I replied, indignantly.

"Then what's the big deal? Planet Shoshanna and the — what do you call them? — the Satellite Girls will give you and me the cold shoulder. I don't exactly see that affecting our quality of life, now, do you?"

I shook my head, but I still felt unconvinced. I guess Jac could tell I was uncomfortable. She rested the ball and chain against a locker and placed both her hands on my shoulders in a way that reminded me of my mother.

"Come on, Kat. Snap out of it. This is junior high school, not a presidential election. Forget all about the wrath of Sho, and go call your mom to tell her we're staying after to start the bio project."

Something in me warmed up, and I smiled.

"Okay," I said.

Jac nodded, satisfied and pleased. She

grabbed hold of her cello case and started hauling it down the corridor as I followed.

"Hey, I almost forgot! We got a dog yesterday.

Jac turned around with a delighted smile.

"What? When did this happen? You never said you might get a dog! Where did you get him? Was he a stray? The pound? Oh, Kat, I hope you didn't go to a puppy store, because you know they —"

"It was absolutely cosmic, Jac. Like he found us. There was a flyer my mom saw — these people were leaving town right away — and, like, an hour later he was at our house. This amazing German shepherd. His name is Max. And it's like he's always lived there."

"I can. Not. Wait. To see him," Jac said. "Oh, Kat, it's like he found you! You were meant to have this dog! Which means he's kind of found me, too, since I'm your friend and so he'll sort of be my stepdog, if that's okay. A German shepherd — this is *so* cool!"

I really can't describe how happy it made me that Jac was almost as excited about Max as I was. You know how people sometimes say that a thing warmed their heart? Well, corny as it sounds, Jac's reaction to the news about Max warmed mine.

"You'll have to come over!" I blurted out, having temporarily forgotten what happened when I invited people to my house.

"Definitely! I cannot wait. I love Max already. We'll walk him, and brush him, and make fun of Shoshanna's Dance Decoration Committee. Maybe we can teach him to growl whenever he hears her name — wouldn't that be hysterical? Silly Kit Kat. What kind of terrible thing did you think was going to happen if you crossed that girl, anyway?"

I would find out the answer to that question in very short order.

The whole thing took under two minutes. I was alone at my locker just before final bell, getting my books together. My mother had given me permission to stay after school in the library with Jac and to bring Jac home with me to meet Max afterward. I was still glowing with pleasure that a simple request to spend time with a new friend could make her so happy. She had known how lonely I was, though I didn't often talk about it. And I knew she felt responsible, moving me to a new town and school where I didn't know anybody.

The girl seemed to come out of nowhere,

like an asteroid suddenly whizzing into the atmosphere and bursting into flames. Brooklyn Bigelow — one of the girls who spent her waking days orbiting Shoshanna. A founding member of the Satellite Girls, and far and away the most vicious one.

Brooklyn didn't say a word as I closed my locker. I took a generous amount of time closing the lock and spinning the dial. When I couldn't think of anything else to do, I turned and looked at her. She was just standing there, her arms folded over her chest, her eyes small and mean. She wasn't an especially pretty girl, but she spent an enormous amount of time and money enhancing, glossing, and coloring everything she had. Brooklyn Bigelow might have been plain in another reality, but in this one she carried herself like a celebrity. Hair an expensively colored and multihued mix of ash blond and lemon. Skin glowing from weekly facials. Her solid frame adorned in the finest and most beautifully tailored clothes. In other words, she was going for the teen celeb look. Expensive.

I wasn't going to initiate a conversation in the face of Brooklyn's open hostility. Nor was I going to flee in fear. So I just stood and stared back at her. To my surprise, she extended the elegantly manicured index finger of her right hand and poked me lightly in the sternum.

"Why, if it isn't the girl who's too busy and important to help out the Dance Decoration Committee. Don't think you can keep it all quiet anymore," Brooklyn said, the index finger jabbing me for emphasis.

"Keep what all quiet?" I asked in spite of myself. Apparently my refusal to do drudge work for the DDC gave Brooklyn license to bring up that "yesterday" bit of ghostly gossip. But I was entirely unprepared for what came next.

"Oh, I think you know exactly what I mean," Brooklyn said. "I'm talking about your mother."

She said the word *mother* like it was an ugly, vile thing. Like *zit.* Like *tumor.* Like *polyester.*

I stood, my face remaining impassive, but my heart began to beat more rapidly. How much did Brooklyn actually know about my mother?

"I've heard a few things," Brooklyn continued, with evident pride, "about what goes on in your house. So I did some asking around. Some people say she's one of those New Age witch types. Spells and chants and whatever. Is that right, Kat? Does she wear a little turban and charge the neighbors five bucks to look into her crystal ball? Does she make voodoo dolls? Love potions? God, I almost feel sorry for you. What's it like, having a freak for a mom?"

I could feel how flushed my face had become, and hot tears filled my eyes. Brooklyn's face was so snide and ugly, it made me feel sick to my stomach.

There were so many things I could have said. I could have told Brooklyn that when she spoke with such self-righteous indignation and nastiness, her face scrunched up and made her look like she was trying to swallow a cube. I could have stared through her and walked right on by as if nothing had passed between us. I could have laughed and told her to knock herself out.

But instead I found myself paralyzed, clutching my book bag and looking in the direction of Brooklyn's feet, praying she was finished and would walk away before I started crying. I heard footsteps, peals of laughter, and the Satellite Girls' familiar voices. The little group slowed down as they neared me. Shoshanna was with them, though she was hanging back. She looked different, somehow. She may have told Brooklyn what happened at my house, but for some reason she wasn't jumping on the trash-Kat wagon now.

"Gosh, Shoshanna, what's the matter? Are you sick?" Brooklyn's fake concerned voice rang up and down the corridor. The Satellite Girls laughed, eager to watch something unfold. But Shoshanna started walking away. Brooklyn hesitated, then trotted after Shoshanna.

"Freak," Brooklyn called to me over her shoulder as she swept past. And for once I thought that maybe Brooklyn was right.

Chapter 6

I was relieved to have someplace to go after the attack of the Satellite Girl, something to distract me. I met Jac in the library as we had planned. It would have been nice to tell Jac what went on, but I couldn't do that without explaining what Brooklyn was talking about, and I wasn't ready to get into the whole "Shoshanna had a bad paranormal experience at my spirit-filled house" thing. So we just joked around instead.

Jac had nabbed us a great table all the way at the back of the library, screened from the librarian and other students by the Reference and Local History stacks. We did plan to work on the bio project, of course, but it was also the first time Jac and I had hung out together outside of the cafeteria. Jac was doing a horrifyingly accurate imitation of Shoshanna bearing down on me with her clipboard, striding toward our table, and tossing her hair as she tapped one finger on an imaginary clipboard. I was laughing so hard I had tears coming out of my eyes. Then I heard a light thud. Jac stopped midstride, looking around.

"What in the world was that?" she asked.

A fat green hardcover book had slid itself out of the top shelf of the closest stack and hurtled to the floor.

It was an accident, I told myself. An innocent shift in the stack that dislodged a loose book. Nothing like a levitating Cornish game hen, or anything of a supernatural ilk. The book had just fallen out of the shelf for no reason. It was certainly not anything weird or unusual, like, say, a communication from the undead. I told myself all this because I had no intention of accepting any reality that involved the undead right now.

"Something fell," I replied, becoming very interested in my bio textbook, which I opened. I rapidly flipped through the pages.

"It was that book," Jac said, pointing at the green hardcover on the floor.

"Maybe," I said, staring at a section in my textbook on cellular division.

Jac picked the green book up and tossed it on the table directly in front of me.

"Don't 'maybe' me," she said. "It was this book. It fell out of the shelf and onto the floor. Weird."

"I'll put it back, then," I said.

I got up and shoved the green book back onto the shelf without looking to see what the title was. When I sat back down at the table, Jac was sitting crossed-legged in her chair watching me, the expression in her green eyes unreadable.

"What?" I asked, suddenly defensive.

"We're friends, aren't we?" Jac asked.

My defensiveness melted rapidly into an inner puddle.

"Of course we are!" I exclaimed.

"Real friends, not like the Satellite Girls are with Shoshanna, right?" Jac pressed.

"Yeah, no!" I said. "Yeah, I mean real friends, Jac. Yes. Absolutely."

"That's what I thought," Jac said, now appearing to become mildly interested in the cover of her own bio textbook. "Because I've been feeling like if I needed to tell you something, or I wanted to, you know, tell you something about myself . . . that I could. Trust you, that is. That it wouldn't change our being friends."

I instantly felt there was nothing Jac could tell me about herself that would make me want to stop being her friend. And I realized she might feel the same way about me. But nobody could possibly have a secret as strange as mine.

"It's just . . . my cello thing. You know, that teacher I told you we moved here for?" Jac said, coloring in an *O* on the cover of her textbook with blue ink.

"Right . . . ," I said, encouraging her.

Whatever she was about to say was interrupted by another thud. I knew what it was before looking at the floor. The green book had fallen again. Specifically, it had thrown itself at my feet.

Good grief. The undead can be down-right pesky sometimes.

"Whoa," said Jac. "Was that . . . is that the same book that fell a minute ago?"

I couldn't exactly pretend I didn't know. Neither of us was stupid. I nodded.

"Okay," Jac continued, peering intently at the book. "Is it just me, or is that creepy?"

I sighed. Here it came — the Shoshanna experience all over again.

"It isn't just you, Jac. It *is* creepy."

The pause that followed was like a huge canyon, one I was stuck at the bottom of, trying to figure how to claw my way out.

"The thing is, Jac, weird things happen around me every once in a while. I seem to . . . attract them, or something." Maybe I could get away with telling her that little snippet and leaving it at that.

Jac looked from the book back to me.

"Okay," she said, carefully. "What do you do?"

"What do I do when?"

"When the weird things happen. Should we just put the book back again?"

I could have sworn at that point that the green book moved, maybe just an inch or so, in my direction. A little hop. I think Jac saw it, too. To her credit, she said nothing.

"Well," I said, "I guess the thing to do is have a look. Maybe it's a lonely book. Maybe it just feels unread."

Jac laughed, and a little of my anxiety went away. I leaned over, picked up the book, and placed it on the table in front of me. Jac pulled her chair closer to mine so we could both see. The cover of the book had our school seal on it.

Jac traced her finger over the cover's raised, faded lettering.

"Nineteen sixty," she read.

"Nineteen sixty," I repeated. "It's an old school yearbook."

I opened the book and began flipping through the pages. The first section was black-and-white photos of graduating seniors, each one with a small, square headshot.

"Look at her hair!" Jac exclaimed, pointing at one of the pictures, "with that dippity-doo flip on the bottom. You could store pencils in that curl!"

"What about the glasses?" I asked, pointing to the same distinguished individual. "What are those, cat's-eye glasses? Like from that cartoon?"

"That girl's wearing them, too!" Jac said, laughing as she pointed to a picture at the bottom of the page. "Do you think someday people in the future will look at our yearbook and laugh at our hair and think *we* look like cartoons?"

"No way," I scoffed, turning to the next page. "People got all the bizarre styles out of their systems in the fifties and sixties. And seventies. And a little in the eighties. We're normal now."

"Yeah, unless you consider boys wearing pants four sizes too big with their underwear hanging out bizarre," said Jac. "These boys all look like military cadets with those crew cuts. Or the band from that video where the singer is playing every part? And he's wearing, like, a cardigan sweater?"

I lifted my hand off the book for a moment to push my hair out of my face. As I did, the book's stiff spine protested, and the book tried to close itself as a hunk of pages flopped to the left.

"You lost our place," Jac said. "I want to see dippity-doo girl again."

She began flipping back to the early pages.

"Every girl in here is a dippity-doo girl," I said.

"Or a beehive girl," Jac added, still flipping pages. "What were they thinking? Did this girl slip on those cat's-eye glasses every morning, pat her big fat beehive hair down in place, and think 'Now I look goooooood?'"

"Maybe their mothers made them," I said, laughing.

"Norma Jean, where are your glasses?" Jac demanded, in a nasally mother voice. "You look darling in those glasses, young lady, and you're darn well going to put them on."

"You need at least three inches of curl, Norma Jean, or no decent boy will ever want to take you on a date," I added, in the same voice.

Maybe it wasn't *that* funny, but Jac and I were howling with laughter like we'd never heard anything so hilarious. I was wiping a tear out of my eye when I noticed the pages ruffling again.

"There goes our place —," Jac began. Then she abruptly stopped.

The book was opening to a different place, but no sane person could blame it on the old, stiff spine of a volume that hadn't been cracked in decades. The pages were turning. One at a time, they were turning. *By themselves.* It was eerie. Like that pack of cards in *Alice in Wonderland.* Some things just weren't supposed to shuffle under their own power.

"Is this another one of those 'weird

things' that sometimes happen when you're around?" Jac whispered.

I nodded, wishing as hard as I could that the pages would stop their spooky little march. And just then, they did.

The book lay open before us, suddenly looking as innocent as any other library book that had never removed itself from a shelf, tap-danced around on the floor, and displayed its own pages one at a time.

"Is it done?" asked Jac, still whispering.

"I think so."

My eye was drawn to a right-hand page of the book. I was staring at it so intently I couldn't make it out. I felt like I was trying to awaken from a dream. After a moment I shifted my gaze a little, and the page came into focus.

It was a full-page photograph of a girl

holding a flute. Though her clothes looked distinctly outdated, the girl in the picture had none of the obvious old-timey style about her that Jac and I had been laughing about. She wore her pale blond hair in two thick, long braids. No glasses. Everything about her was skinny and angular. Her fingers were bony, her wrists tiny and delicate, even her neck seemed too long and thin. Her face was all lines and angles, too, which made her eyes look like they belonged to a different face because they were so huge and deep. Though it was an old picture, a little grainy and not in color, I had a feeling the girl's complexion was unusually pale. There was a hint of a shadow under each eye. She was holding the flute to her lips and obviously playing or pretending to, her eyes looking off to the left. The girl wore a cardigan sweater buttoned up to the top and a long, full skirt that, even to my amateur's eye, looked like it might be a few years out of date for the times. The fabric of both skirt and sweater seemed worn, like hand-me-downs. Looking closer, I could see that both of the elbows in the sweater had been worn practically through. Her clothing didn't seem to have any particular color to it. I guessed maybe sweater and skirt might have been gray.

"'In memoriam,'" I heard Jac say, and my eyes fell on the words as she read them.

"'In memoriam,'" I murmured, not realizing I was saying it out loud until I heard my own voice. "'In loving memory of Suzanne Bennis, 1943–1960.'"

"Geez, she died?" asked Jac, though it wasn't really a question. There it was, laid out in front of us in black and white. A student named Suzanne Bennis, who played the flute and hadn't updated her wardrobe in quite some time, had died when she was only seventeen years old.

"It must have happened during the school year," I said. "They had students all the way through high school in this building back then. She might have been a junior or a senior."

"It doesn't say how she died," Jac said. "Don't they think that's important? It makes a difference."

I didn't know what Jac meant by it making a difference, but I also wanted to know how this pretty but tired-looking girl had died. It made me kind of sad to think about it.

Jac made a funny little sound, something between a sigh and a meow. I looked at her to see if she might be crying or something, but she was just studying the page intently, tracing Suzanne Bennis's outline with her finger. She had her head bent over the yearbook like she was looking into a microscope. I was wondering if she might have spotted something in the picture I'd missed, and I was trying to look over her shoulder when I realized all at once that there was someone standing behind Jac.

Let me clarify. It wasn't so much that I realized it all at once. It was more like one second there was no one there, and the next second there was. It happened in about the time it took to blink. I refused to take my gaze off of Jac's face, and she was still absorbed in the yearbook. I simply would not look behind her. I just wouldn't. But I felt a buzz in the area, like an electrical charge.

Even without directly looking, I could see a couple of things in my peripheral vision. One was a long, full skirt. The other was the ends of two pale fat braids, hanging just behind Jac's head. I knew what was there. Or who was there. It was Suzanne Bennis. Suzanne Bennis, who had played the flute and had been dead for almost fifty years. She was standing very straight and still, her hands clasped in front of her. She might have been staring down at the yearbook, I wasn't sure. I could see a frayed gray elbow of a sweater. She was dressed in the same clothes she wore in the yearbook picture, and she was just as motionless.

I closed my eyes and felt sick to my stomach. It was bad enough seeing spirits on the street. But in school? In the *library?* It was like an express ticket to the outcast table. Forget lunch, it was like an express ticket to the school counselor. To mental health evaluations. What if I started seeing spirits on the bus? What if I started seeing them in *homeroom?*

I needed time to figure out how to deal. I just needed a little time.

"Please, not now, please, not now," I whispered. "Just not now . . ."

"Not now what?" Jac asked. "Kat? Are you okay?"

I couldn't sit there with my eyes closed like I was in a yoga class or something. I opened them partway and squinted at Jac.

"Are you okay?" she repeated.

I wasn't sure, but through my squint I no longer saw the braids behind Jac. I opened my eyes all the way. I couldn't help but breathe a sigh of relief. Suzanne Bennis was gone. Whether she'd just blinked out or she'd heard my plea and gone away, she was most definitely gone.

"I'm fine," I said to Jac.

"You're sure?" Jac asked. She was running her hand up and down her arm, which I could see was covered in goose bumps.

"I'm sure," I answered.

"Positive?"

I let out a huge breath. "Yes, Jac, I am positive!"

"That's good," Jac said. "In that case, I'm ready."

"You're ready for what?"

Jac pushed the book toward me with both hands.

"I'm ready for you to tell me exactly what just happened here."

Chapter 7

There was no way out of it. I knew that. If I wanted to keep Jac as my friend, I needed to be straight with her. Not just about weird things happening, but about the whole thing. My mom being a medium. Me having spirit sight. The undead hanging around, tugging at my shirtsleeves. All of it. Whether she'd still feel comfortable around me after knowing the truth was out of my control.

"Okay," I said. "Okay. I'll tell you. But not here. My mom said we could go to my house if we had time, remember? Let's go."

"Sure," Jac said. "I'll get to see Max. It is just flat-out crazy how excited I am that *you* got a dog. Does he wear a red bandanna around his neck?"

I laughed as I put my books and pen into my book bag and checked the library table to make sure I wasn't forgetting anything.

"Well, he didn't come with one, Jac. But who knows. If we scrounge one up, maybe he'll tolerate wearing it."

"Before we moved, my room looked over this park where everybody brought their dogs," Jac said. "And the smartest, most beautiful dog, I think it was a border collie or something, would come catch a Frisbee with his owner every day. You can't believe how gorgeous this dog was. And he wore this red bandanna around his neck. I was so jealous of the guy who owned him. And there was also this woman who came every day with her three beagles. Three! I would have settled for one little dog, a little tiny one, I wouldn't have cared. But I stopped asking for a dog a long time ago. My mother takes it so . . . personally. Like I'm asking her to . . . I don't know. Shave her head or something. And she tells me that it is *simply impossible* for our family to ever get another dog."

"Why?"

"She says it's allergies, but really it's a control thing. There's no way she could tolerate so much as one dog hair on her floors."

It was sweet, thinking of Jac wanting Max to wear a red bandanna like the dog she used to watch playing Frisbee, but it was also kind of sad. And her mother sounded, well . . . not so much fun.

"Max'll be *our* dog, Jac. We'll totally share him. Come on, let's go see him."

We headed out of the library and down

the hallway for the side exit by the parking lot, Jac dragging her ball and chain behind her. We had almost made it outside when I heard an unpleasantly familiar voice calling to me.

"Kat, are you done with that bio project? Because it would be fab if you could go ahead and work on those decorations now. I have to leave early because of a family . . . thing."

I turned reluctantly. Shoshanna was standing all the way at the other end of the hall. A Satellite Girl I didn't recognize was standing behind her, looming a good six inches taller.

"I really need everyone to step up to the plate right now."

"Kat," Jac murmured, "come on. Let's go."

I seemed to be stuck standing there with my feet glued in place. It was like one of those dreams when the bad guy is chasing you and you can't run away.

"Please, Kat!" Shoshanna called.

Shoshanna never said please. I registered this as she took a step down the hallway toward me, so that I could see the girl behind her. She was tall and painfully thin, in a fraying sweater and skirt. Her intensely pale face was framed by two white-blond, fat braids.

Suzanne Bennis stared at me from the end of the hallway. And I knew instinctively that she wanted to tell me something. That she needed my help. I was afraid. Of what she wanted from me.

"No!" I said, quickly. "I'm not ready! Not now!! Give me some *time!*"

"Time for *what?*" I heard Shoshanna call. But my feet had come unstuck, and I grabbed Jac's arm and pulled her out the door. I felt in my heart that Suzanne Bennis would not follow us outside. That her territory was the school, or certain parts of it. Still, as Jac and I reached the sidewalk and started walking briskly toward my house, I didn't look back. We couldn't walk as fast as I wanted to with Jac pulling her cello, but there wasn't anything to be done about that.

"So, that was an *interesting* way to deal with Shoshanna," Jac said. "A little odd, but interesting."

I sighed. There was no time, apparently, like the present. Maybe talking while we walked would be easier. I wouldn't have to look into those green eyes, possibly seeing them go wide with terror.

"I wasn't talking to Shoshanna," I said. "I was, uh, talking to Suzanne."

"Who's Suzanne?" asked Jac, chattily.

"Okay," I said, staring straight ahead and walking purposefully. "Here's the thing, Jac. I kind of see dead people."

Chapter 8

"You see dead people," Jac repeated, like she was making sure she had a correct street address. "Like the kid in that movie?"

"Like the kid in that movie, yes. It's not . . . I haven't . . . See, my mom does. My mom is a medium."

"Like that TV show?"

Good grief, did Jac have to translate *everything* into pop culture terms? But she was right.

"Like that, yes. Basically. I've grown up with it. I'm used to it. Used to it happening to her, that is. It's just who she is. Like some moms are neat freaks, or aerobics instructors."

"Or lawyers," Jac added helpfully.

"Yeah. It's just what she is, what she does, or whatever. But the thing is, Jac, when I turned thirteen a few months ago, it started happening to *me*."

Jac came to a full stop, so I had to also. I turned to look at her. The ball and chain was upright next to her, standing there companionably like an oversized sibling.

"So one day, *blam*, you just started seeing dead people?" Jac asked. She sounded incredulous, and I appreciated that. Since I'd never told anybody about it, I'd never gotten to share how absolutely nutso the experience is.

"Exactly. I'm still getting used to it. And the thing is, you can't do anything about it.

You can't just point the remote at them and change the channel. If they're there, they're *there*."

We started walking again.

"What did your mom say?" Jac asked. "She must have been able to give you some good tips."

"Yeah, except I haven't exactly told her," I said.

"You haven't told her?" Jac asked. "Don't you think it would make her happy to know you see dead people, too?"

"I do think it would make *her* happy, yeah," I said. "The thing is, Jac, I'm not sure it makes *me* happy. My mom considers it a gift, totally. I'm more inclined to see it as a burden. That probably sounds so selfish."

"Not at all," Jac said. "Believe me, I hear you one hundred percent."

"You're the only person I've ever told," I

said. "I don't mean just about me. About my mom, too."

I hadn't even realized that was true until I said it. I had never confided in anyone my own age that my mother was a medium. Girls I knew at my old school were certainly aware that my mom was a New Age type, but I let them think her work was more, like, healing stuff. Tarot cards, which she actually does read. Energy stuff. Aura reading. I snuck a peek at Jac. She was not hightailing it down the sidewalk. She was not staring at me in horror. She looked pretty much like she always looked, except she seemed to be mulling something over.

"Oh, my gosh," she said suddenly. "You saw Suzanne Bennis back there, didn't you?"

This girl was sharp. More importantly, she wasn't freaking out. Now I could finally put all my cards on the table.

"Yep," I said.

"Where?" Jac asked. "How? What did she look like? Tell me everything!"

"Well, first I saw her in the library, when we were looking at her picture. She was . . ." Jac was doing so well in the calm department I didn't want to rattle her by telling her a spirit had been standing right behind her, close enough to put a pale hand on the back of Jac's neck. Better to modify that information, or save it for later. ". . . she was near that stack where the yearbook came from. She was standing very still, with her hands in front of her. And she looked so thin, Jac, but she's also really tall. Even if she was seventeen, she seemed a good six or eight inches taller than any high school girl I know. And those circles she has under her eyes, like she didn't ever sleep enough."

"And what happened?"

"Nothing. I became aware she was there, and then she was just gone the next second. Like she blinked right out of existence. But when we were in the hallway, leaving, I saw her again, standing right behind Shoshanna."

"Suzanne Bennis was standing behind Shoshanna?" Jac asked, sounding amazed.

I nodded.

Jac made an explosive sound, and I actually took a step back. I didn't know all of Jac's noises yet. But this one turned out to be the prelude to an enormous, gut-wrenching burst of laughter. Jac bent forward and actually stamped her foot on the ground as she laughed.

"Just imagine . . . if she knew . . . an aspiring Satellite Girl from Beyond the Grave . . ."

I started to laugh, too. Jac was being cooler than I ever dreamed possible about all this. This was a girl I might actually be able to have in my home without anxiety. When Jac's laughter had finally faded into a quiet, hiccuppy string of little giggles, I pointed down the street.

"So that's my house, there," I said.

"Great," Jac said, getting a good grip on the ball and chain. "Let's go see Max!"

I let Jac go ahead of me and felt a surge of affection for her as I watched her pull her cello along the uneven sidewalk toward my front door. I was bringing a friend to my home, and I wasn't worried that something paranormal might happen. Jac had taken the news about my spirit sight so matter-of-factly I might as well have told her that my secret was that I took tango lessons on the weekends.

I caught up to her at the front door and opened it. Max was there immediately, looking noble and strong as he strained to express his pleasure at our arrival by the furious wagging of his tail. Jac dropped immediately to her knees to Max's level. He gave her face a gentle sniff, and when he continued to wag his tail, she wrapped her arms around his neck and pressed her face against his fur. "Look at him. He looks like a movie star."

He *was* a handsome dog, I gave her that. Max stood patiently for a few moments as Jac and I petted him and complimented him on his magnificence. Then he trotted down the hallway and turned into the living room.

I helped Jac park her cello against the wall. Because the door at the end of the hall was closed, I knew my mother was probably still in a session, so I took Jac's arm and led her into the living room where Max was already stretched royally on his pillow by the window. Jac made herself at home immediately, plopping down on the worn couch and patting the faded cushions appreciatively.

"Comfy," she said. "My mother would keep the couch covered in plastic if my father would let her."

I plopped down next to Jac. Outside, there was a rumble of thunder and the hissing sound of a sudden strong rainfall on the pavement.

"We got inside just in time," I said. Everything seemed cozy and good.

"I just can't get over you seeing Suzanne Bennis standing behind Shoshanna," Jac said, shaking her head. "Hey, are those cookies for us?"

I reached for the plate my mother had left out and handed it to Jac as another roll of thunder began. She zeroed in on a gingersnap.

"So what happens next?" she asked, turning the cookie over several times and scrutinizing it before taking a bite.

"With Suzanne Bennis?" I asked.

Jac nodded, her mouth full.

"I honestly don't know, Jac. She wants something. She was trying to get my attention, and I just wasn't ready to give it to her. Like I said, I'm really new at this. But I'm going to have to get ready, whatever that means. I just don't know yet."

Jac nodded again, examining her half-eaten cookie with narrowed eyes. Then her mouth widened into a mischievous grin.

"At least the next time Shoshanna asks you where your school spirit is, you'll be able to show her," she remarked, then promptly cracked herself up.

I cracked up, too, laughing as the rain poured down outside and feeling that no matter what happened with Suzanne Bennis, for the moment all was right with the world. Max was snoring softly in the corner. I had a friend, and she knew my freaky secret. And it was cool with her.

It wasn't until much later that night, after I'd gotten into bed, that I remembered Jac had been about to tell me her own secret in the library, and she had never gotten to say what it was.

Chapter 9

The next day was a school holiday — the mysteriously named Superintendent's Day, which to me conjured up images of old men in blue uniforms and matching caps smoking cigars and awarding one another medals. Whatever it actually was, it got us out of school for the entire day, which would have thrilled me under any circumstances. The fact that it gave me an extra day to avoid contact with the restless spirit of Suzanne Bennis was icing on the cake. I was still pretty nervous about how it would go and what I was supposed to do. How do you strike up a conversation with a dead girl, anyway?

Jac wanted to go into town with me to see the local history museum, an idea my mother enthusiastically endorsed. Medford had a small but locally famous contingent of pioneers who in the 1850s set out from the center of town in search of a new home. The museum chronicled life in the area all the way back to prehistoric times, but the pioneers were definitely the stars. Oddly, although Jac's primary nonmusical interest seemed to be very current pop culture, she also had a soft spot for *Little House on the Prairie.* She'd been pitching the idea of going to the museum for days, and I had finally caved.

We rendezvoused at the bus stop mid-morning. Jac was wearing a pale blue oxford button-down with wide-leg beige corduroys and navy Merrell clogs. Over her arm was slung a shiny green raincoat with a strawberry design. It pained me slightly that my new best friend dressed as if she had tumbled off the cover of a Talbot's catalog, but if she was willing to overlook the paranormal cloud surrounding me and mine, I could find a way to deal with her Young Hillary Clinton look.

It was one of the few times I had seen her without the ball and chain in tow. The instrument's absence made her look even smaller and more fragile than usual. But her face looked bright and eager, and she broke into a huge smile when she saw me.

"Yay! You're here! This is so great, Kit Kat. We're going to have a blast. Maybe they'll teach us how to churn butter!"

I hugged her while theorizing how boring her life must be, since her level of excitement was more in keeping with someone who had just scored tickets and backstage passes to a Green Day concert. But I felt a pleasant buzz of anticipation myself, not so much at the idea of perusing the artifacts of our town's founding fathers but to be doing something with Jac that didn't involve school or Shoshanna dodging.

Other than hanging out at my house the night before, this was the first time I'd experienced Jac away from school and away from her cello, in the real world. She was much talkier than I was used to. She was funny, too. I liked it.

"So my aunt sends this note back to my parents reminding them that she'll be away in Bali all next month doing an intensive Pilates/yoga retreat with Rodney Yee . . ."

"Who's Rodney Yee? What kind of a

name is that?" I interrupted as our bus lumbered along.

"He's one of those stud-muffin yoga gurus. I think he trained Cindy Crawford. Anyway, I know because I heard my father talking about it that she isn't going to Bali at all — she's having a knee lift and a toe reduction and she wants to establish her alibi early so no one will suspect."

"Toe reduction?" I exclaimed.

Jac nodded gravely, but her lips twitched.

"She's got these *humongous* clompers, and nothing fits her feet right except for Easy Spirit pumps. She wants to wear money shoes. You know. Like Manillas and Choo Choo's."

"Manolos," I said. "And Jimmy Choos."

What can I say? I read the Styles section in the Sunday *Times* religiously.

"Exactly," Jac said. "But her feet are too big. After the toe shortening and a little heel shave, she's hoping to be able to cram 'em into stilettos."

"That is the most twisted thing I've ever heard," I said. "Oh, this is our stop."

"That's nothing," Jac said as she got to her feet. "She's been a complete nut job ever since she moved to LA. She has a therapist for her *houseplants.*"

I was unable to question Jac about this remarkable statement as I had become distracted by a publicity display outside the museum's front door.

The museum had set up a replica of a covered wagon, complete with a live ox. An actor dressed in what looked like *Little House on the Prairie* wardrobe cast-offs sat on the wagon's seat stiffly.

"I guess business must be extremely

bad, or extremely good, if the museum is advertising with *that*," I said, nudging Jac in the arm and pointing toward the wagon.

"A hot dog stand?" she asked.

"No, genius, with *that*. The covered wagon complete with Captain Pa at the helm."

Jac glanced in the direction I was pointing, then looked back at me.

"Are you joking, or do you see . . . one of your thingies?"

The look I gave Jac clearly indicated it was a thingy sighting. Jac looked discreetly back in its direction.

"Is it doing anything?" she whispered.

As if on cue, Pa cracked a whip into the air and the ox lumbered across two lanes of traffic, pulling the wagon smoothly behind. Cars whizzed straight through the entire spectacle without so much as slowing. I stared with my mouth hanging open as the wagon, Captain Pa, ox, and all disappeared through the wall of a Taco Bell.

"Oh, man," I said. "That is insane."

"Which . . . particular aspect are you referring to?" Jac asked carefully. We were still standing in the middle of the sidewalk where the bus had let us off.

"Just the unexpectedness of it. I don't know how to get used to these random specters just blinking in and out of my personal space. Here I am blabbing to you about it because I think it's really there. I mean, what if I'd been with someone else? Someone who . . . you know. Doesn't *know* about me."

Jac squeezed my arm.

"You aren't with someone else. You're with me. And you'll get used to all this eventually. Come on — let's go inside."

I nodded and smiled and followed Jac to the museum entrance. On the way in, I glanced over at the place where I'd seen the wagon. There was nothing there but the hot dog vendor, who looked blissfully unaware of his recent brush with history.

Was this my life now? Was I going to be seeing the undead walking and talking and violating the laws of physics in neighborhood fast-food establishments every day? And to think I had once worried about looking cool. It was becoming increasingly obvious that my problem should be not how to look cool, but how *not* to look like a deranged, hallucinating nut job.

Inside the museum, we cruised through Early Farm Life, unimpressed by the pitchfork collection and diorama on the four stages of stump removal. Jac seemed strangely interested in an illustrated account of sheepshearing until she noticed the display of dried locusts in the next case.

"Gross!" she squealed, jumping back and crashing into me. The force of her locust phobia brought us both to the ground, where we sat stunned and giggling. Her strawberry-covered rain slicker lay in a terrified heap at her feet.

"Chill out, Jac. Those bugs are dead!" I laughed.

"They're still repulsive," Jac replied, inching farther from the display by sliding on her butt. "Bugs thoroughly and completely freak me out. People have been *hospitalized* for lesser trauma."

I pulled Jac to her feet and led her through the archway to the next exhibit.

"Don't worry," I said. "We'll be safe here in Early Stores and Apothecaries."

I was secretly planning to tickle the back of Jac's neck in my best crawling locust imitation when I noticed we weren't alone in this room. Over in the corner by the apothecary display was a dark-haired girl bent studiously over a notebook. I recognized her immediately as Quinn Irvin, ninth-grade class president and captain of the girls' varsity soccer team. Quinn had achieved fame by the rarefied combination of scholastic excellence, athletic accomplishment, and genuine good-heartedness. Everyone liked Quinn Irvin. Even Shoshanna Longbarrow. I certainly didn't want to look stupid in front of Quinn, so I ended my locust simulation prank and tried to look respectable. I was getting ready to call over to Quinn and wave when I saw a woman sitting on a stool directly behind her. The woman wore a floor-length dress with an apron over it and seemed to be grinding something to powder in a little mortar and pestle. My heart sank.

To make matters worse, Quinn had spotted me and was waving. If I waved back, was nineteenth-century Apothecary Lady going to think I was waving to *her?* There was no way I could have a normal conversation if a dead person was simultaneously trying to get my attention. I mean, come on!

But Quinn was gesturing for us to come over.

I smiled widely as we walked toward Quinn.

"Hi, what's up?" I said, trying to sound as friendly and casual as possible.

"I've got a research project on early American merchants for history," Quinn said. "I'm trying to get a jump on it. Hey, you're the girl who plays cello, right?"

"That's right," replied Jac, sounding pleased. "I'm Jac. It's nice to meet you."

Everything sounded very normal and

civilized, when Jac suddenly leaned around Quinn to where the phantom lady was standing. To my horror, Jac stuck her hand out in the spirit's direction and promptly introduced herself.

"Hi, I'm Jac," she said.

I was utterly horrified. What was Jac doing? What could she possibly be thinking? She was supposed to *ignore* spirit activity, not pretend she could see it!

"Jac, honey, are you having one of your little spells again?" I asked quickly.

Quinn gave me an odd glance before turning in the direction Jac had extended her hand.

"Yeah, I'm sorry. Jac and Kat, this is my mother. Mom, these are two friends from seventh grade."

The woman put down her mortar and pestle, smoothed her apron, and smiled.

"Nice to meet you, girls. Forgive the outfit. I volunteer a few times a week as a living history model for the museum."

Oh, man. I thought I'd hit bottom when I started seeing people who were actually spirits. Now I was seeing spirits who were actually *people*. This had to be a new all-time low in the life of a young medium.

"So, um, we need to get on over to the colonial school exhibit in the other room. Great to see you, Quinn, and nice to meet you, Ms. Irvin."

Jac waited to speak until I'd dragged her to the next room and we were standing safely in front of the light-up display labeled Dunce Caps Throughout the Years.

"You want to clue me in?" she asked. "One of my little spells?"

I gave the deep sigh of one who has been entirely overspent in the supernatural arena.

"When I saw that woman in those old-timey clothes I just assumed she was another ghost. And then you went and introduced yourself to her, and honestly, Jac, I didn't know what was going on. For a minute I wasn't sure who was alive and who wasn't. I honestly don't think I can do this."

"Do what?"

"Be a medium."

Jac looked thoughtful.

"Well, is there some kind of cancellation policy? Is there some person who can . . . remove it?"

I stared at my friend bleakly.

"No. It isn't a wart. It's a gift."

"Yeah," Jac said. "Well, I guess that's that, then."

Tell me something I didn't already know. I might as well say I could no longer handle the stress of time, space, and gravity. Options were simply not available.

I glanced around the room to make sure we were still alone, and my eyes registered some kind of movement through the door in the room beyond. There was no way I was going to wait around to categorize it as man or myth.

"Can we get out of here? I'm getting creeped out. There's supposed to be a garden out back. We can eat our sandwiches there."

Jac peered in the direction of the door marked EXIT where a garden and tables were partially visible.

"Will there be bees?" she asked nervously.

I took her by the arm and pulled her to the exit.

"I will personally throw myself in between you and any bee, wasp, locust, or ladybug, dead or alive, that dares to approach you."

I relaxed a little when we got into the sunny garden. We were the only people there, and we found a nice table by a little fountain. Everything seemed normal again in the light of day. I unwrapped the sandwich my mother had made for me, took a bite, and watched Jac methodically take apart her sandwich and put it back together again.

"Just checking," she said. I decided not to ask what exactly she was checking for.

We munched in silence for a few minutes and I mopped up a puddle of my soda, which had exploded in an unexpected instance of beverage revenge.

"Hey, Jac? You know when were in the library? Right before the Suzanne Bennis thing happened?"

Jac peered at me over her reconstructed sandwich and nodded as she took a bite.

"You were about to tell me something. About your cello. Or maybe it was your cello teacher. Remember?"

Jac continued chewing, but more slowly.

"Yeah," she said after a moment.

"Not that you have to say anything," I added quickly. "If you don't want to or you changed your mind or whatever."

"No," Jac replied. "I haven't changed my mind. With your spook circus going on, I actually forgot about it for a while."

I waited patiently as Jac finished her sandwich and daintily patted her lips with a napkin.

"My cello, yeah," Jac said finally. "Things are not exactly . . . as I've represented them. Not entirely."

What was Jac getting at? That she'd been

faking? That she wasn't really a cellist at all and just dragged the case around filled with . . . what? Insect repellent?

"Okay, the thing is this. I don't exactly play the cello anymore. I mean, I've kind of mostly stopped altogether. And my mother doesn't know. I'm supposed to practice every day before school in the music room for two hours, see, because we live in an apartment complex and people will theoretically complain if I practice too much there. I've been lugging my cello to school every day because obviously my parents would notice if I left it at home. But when I get to school early, I just do homework or read in the music room. Stare into space. I don't practice."

Now, frankly, this did not sound like much of a confession to me. So far, "I don't practice the cello" wasn't ranking equally with "I see dead people." But Jac looked like she had more to say, and I had plenty of time on my hands. My face must have looked kind of blank, because Jac decided more details were necessary.

"You know, I think I need to start a little further back. I've been playing the cello since I was four years old, and I don't mean single-note versions of "Twinkle, Twinkle" and "Old MacDonald." I was way *advanced.* From the beginning. And my mother, she was like one of those stage moms dragging the kid to auditions and beauty pageants when they're still in pull-ups. Except with music. She took my playing super seriously. I didn't do anything else, no sports, no dancing, no Mommy and Me or Gymboree. When I wasn't having lessons, I was practicing. And it paid off. I got, you know, good. Kind of insanely good. I was performing in professional concerts, with orchestras, when I was, like, eight or nine. Doing competitions. Young Musicians series. Stuff like that."

Wow. I waited for Jac to go on. She was so focused on the story, she didn't even notice a bumblebee buzzing lazily around the table.

"So last year, this is before we moved here, my mother's wheeling and dealing ended up in the holy grail of classical music, at least in her opinion. She got me a spot in this Young Artists benefit performance at Carnegie Hall. You know, *the* Carnegie Hall. In New York City. It was what she'd wanted for herself, all her life, when she was still playing."

"Your mom plays the cello, too?" I asked.

"The viola, actually. But yeah. She's a failed virtuoso of the first order, taking a life's worth of disappointment out on me. But that's another story. In concerts like that, you only have one or two sessions the day before to rehearse onstage with the orchestra. I practiced for months, day in, day out. But when I got to the rehearsal and had to play my solo, I choked."

Jac paused.

"Choked, like on a peach pit?" I prompted helpfully.

"Choked. Froze. Tanked."

"You didn't play well?" I asked.

"I didn't play at *all,*" Jac explained. "Not a single note. It was like I was paralyzed, except that my hands shook. I saw spots. Not so much stage fright as stage *terror.*"

"Oh, man. I guess your mother was pretty mad."

"She was *apoplectic,*" Jac exclaimed.

I had never heard the word *apoplectic* before, but from the way it sounded and the look on Jac's face when she said it, I had a good idea of what it meant. I got a sudden visual flash of a generic-looking mother with a bright red face and steam literally shooting out of her ears.

"Yikes," I said.

"And it never went away," Jac continued. "I just couldn't play. They ended up having to pull me from the benefit and replace me with some prodigy kettle-drum player. And I haven't been able to play since."

"Not at all?" I asked.

Jac shook her head.

"Not if anyone is there. Anyone. Even a cello teacher. I can only play if I'm alone. Like, entirely alone with no possibility of anyone overhearing. Even then, it isn't like it was. I don't have what I used to have. The music doesn't come from the same place. I don't know, it's hard to describe."

In the doorway to the museum, I caught

a glimpse of an elderly woman wearing a sunbonnet standing next to a young Native American boy clad in buckskin. Without even realizing what I was doing, I made eye contact with the woman and shook my head sharply, mouthing *no* for emphasis. To my astonishment, the duo instantly disappeared.

"But there was no way my mother was going to let me stop," Jac said. "When it became obvious by that summer that I wasn't getting any better, she started researching teachers who specialize in getting students to overcome stage fright. Somehow she heard about Miss Wittencourt. And that's why I'm here."

"Your family really picked up and moved across the state just so you could be near a cello teacher?" I asked, astonished.

Jac nodded glumly.

"I know, no pressure, right? That's why

we moved midyear. Once she found Miss Wittencourt and as soon as she located an apartment, *blam.* We were gone."

"And you've been here how long?" I asked.

"Seven weeks," Jac said. "And in that time, I have practiced the cello exactly zero times. I take it with me to school, like my mother says. I sit with it in the music room when the rest of the world is getting out of bed and brushing their teeth, like my mother says. But I haven't played so much as a scale."

"Well, what about your teacher?" I asked.

Jac shrugged.

"I don't know what to tell you. Twice a week, plus every other Saturday morning, I go there. I sit. She sits. The cello sits. Nothing. It's like she's waiting for something to happen, but it never does."

"And she doesn't say anything?"

"Just a few words. 'Hello. How are you feeling?' 'Would you like a glass of iced tea?' 'Goodbye.' And at the start of each lesson, she always asks, 'And what are we going do today, Miss Jacqueline?'"

"'Miss Jacqueline?'"

"'Miss Jacqueline.' No nickname, and whatever you do, don't say 'Ms.' The woman is old-fashioned. She's Miss Wittencourt and I'm Miss Jacqueline. So she asks, and I shrug, and that's it. We just sit there."

"Well, what does your mother say?"

"She doesn't say anything. Which can only mean one thing. Miss Wittencourt hasn't mentioned this little detail to her — that I don't actually *play* during our lessons."

Now, this seemed odd.

"Well, do you think she's . . . scamming you?" I asked cautiously.

Jac shook her head.

"I don't think so," she said. "I don't know what she's doing. But I've gotten there early a few times and heard the student before me. Violin player. Rocks the roof off the house. So clearly the woman is *capable* of teaching. She's just choosing not to teach *me.*"

Jac paused and finally became aware of the bumblebee, which was still lurking around the table. She gave a little shriek and put her hands up in front of her face. The bee, strangely understanding, buzzed off.

"It's gone," I said. Jac took her hands away from her face and looked around cautiously. Then she looked at me.

"You're the only one I've told," she said. "Nobody else knows. Nobody."

"I won't say anything," I reassured her.

Jac gave me a grateful look.

"Likewise," she said. "So . . . do you think I'm crazy?"

I rolled my eyes.

"Jac, can you sit there in all honesty and ask a reluctant medium if she thinks a cellist with stage fright is crazy?"

Jac laughed.

"No," she replied. "I guess not. So we're quite a pair."

"Quite," I repeated. "Whatever will become of us?"

"Well, at least you have a logical option," Jac said.

I raised one eyebrow at Jac. "What are you talking about?"

"I'm talking about it being very clear what you ought to do next, Kat."

I waited.

"You need to talk to a pro. Kat, you need to tell your mother."

Chapter 10

I gave Jac's suggestion a lot of thought and came to the conclusion that she was right. My spirit sight wasn't going to go away, at least not anytime soon. And neither was my mom. It was time for me to broach the topic with her. But how to start? How did anyone start on that subject?

There should be a phone service, I thought, something like 1-800-MEDIUM1. Where an automated voice would direct you.

Press one if an object in your home is levitating.

Press two if there is ectoplasm oozing out of your walls.

Press three if spirits are disrupting your cable service.

Press four if you've inherited your mother's psychic abilities.

To speak to a medium, press zero.

Zero. Zero. Zero.

I waited until after dinner that night. My mom was in her usual state of quiet contentment. As she wrapped the remainder of the tofu and mozzarella casserole and put it away, Max watched hopefully, waiting for a stray bite that never fell.

But just as I was getting ready to start things off, the phone rang. She answered it and listened in silence for a few moments.

"I understand. And this was your mother's mother? Yes, I see. Actually, I'm just finishing dinner here with my daughter, Kat."

Something about the way she said *daughter,* followed by my name, gave me the feeling she didn't want to talk to this person with me around.

"Right, yes. That'll be fine. Talk to you then."

My mother didn't offer any explanation when she hung up. Usually, we were totally not the type to pry into each other's business. If it came up, it came up. If it didn't, you didn't ask. But my curiosity got the better of me.

"Who was that?" I asked.

"The usual. Someone needing help," she said. "Did you and Jac have fun today? How was the museum?"

This was probably as good an opening as any. I sat down at the kitchen table, which I'd wiped clean a few minutes ago. My mother sat down across the table from me, reaching over to light the big beeswax candle. She seemed to sense something was up. Of course she did.

"The museum was fine," I said. "Not all that exciting. At least, it shouldn't have been. Wasn't, for those lucky *normal* people."

My mother nodded as if what I'd just said made sense. I knew there was no lengthy backstory necessary here.

"I've started to see them, Mom," I said.

The room seemed to blink out for a fraction of a second, like when you're watching television and the signal goes off during a thunderstorm. My mother was staring at me across the table. Her face looked strangely lined in the flickering of the single candle.

"Yes," she said. "Was it your birthday?"

She knew. Of course, she already knew.

I nodded.

"At first it was just a random sighting

here and there, you know. But something's happened, Mom. It's like my whole system is getting amped up, and I'm starting to see them *everywhere.* Like, all the time."

My mother turned her necklace over and over in her hand.

"When did that start? You seeing them so frequently?"

"Today," I said. "I can't . . . I just don't think I can do this."

I suddenly felt like crying. I felt like a baby, a first-grader coming home from school to complain that military-style push-ups were now required in gym, that no one seemed to understand I was just a kid, that it was just too *hard*, and how could something so adult be expected of me?

"You saw the elderly gentleman in black that night we walked to the river," she said.

I nodded, and almost asked how she knew. But, duh. She knew because she saw him, too.

"And a few before that. Just on the street, you know. And something in school I'll tell you about in a minute. But today, Mom, I saw enough spirits that I started to not be able to tell the difference between the dead people and the living ones. It's like it's getting *worse*. If this is what it's going to be like, I just don't know how to handle it."

"Oh, Kat," my mom said, reaching for my hand over the tabletop. "Honey. First of all, it isn't getting worse. You have to realize where you were."

"Where I was?"

"You were in a *museum*," she said. "A place full of old objects that used to belong to someone. There are certain places that act almost as spirit magnets. Graveyards, hospitals, theaters. And museums. The sight doesn't accelerate, Kat. You just happened to be in a place chock-full of ghosts."

Now *that* was a relief. Seriously. There was nothing like finding out you're not going to see boatloads of ghosts all the time to make the prospect of seeing ghosts *periodically* seem more dealable.

"I'm sorry," I said suddenly. "I should have told you right away, I know. It's just, I'm not so sure I'm completely thrilled about this. And I know you love being a medium, and I didn't want to make you feel bad by being such a baby about it . . ."

"You're not being a baby, and you couldn't possibly make me feel bad," my mother said. "Kat, coming into the sight is complicated. It's a gift that requires a great deal of fortitude and sacrifice. It takes a long time to get comfortable with it. Some people never do."

"I'm just not sure how to deal with it. I don't know what's expected of me. I'm in seventh grade, remember. Where you're supposed to spend every waking hour trying to be *normal*. This is so . . . so *not* normal."

"You're right," she replied. "It's not. But in reality, Kat, and you're probably too young to know this, but in reality there is no normal. Normal is something people have agreed to invent so we have something to compare ourselves to. Normal should be the least of your worries, sweetie."

Easy for *her* to say. She had rocketed out of the realms of normal ages ago.

"It's just . . . what am I supposed to do?"

I asked. "Is there some kind of instruction manual? A tutorial, maybe? Because I'm flying blind here."

My mother laughed.

"There's me," she said. "I can help you. We can talk about things, or I can read your cards for you. But you have everything you need within you. Your intuition is your instruction manual. You're seeing spirits now. That's how it begins. And it seems bizarre, and it's jarring at first, but trust me when I tell you that you *will* get used to it. There will come a time when it will seem strange that *everyone* doesn't see what you do."

We'll see about that.

"All you need to do now is watch and wait," she continued. "Get used to the sight. You don't have to do anything else. Not yet. In time, you'll go on to the next step."

"Which is?" I asked.

"You'll be approached by a spirit," she said. "You'll be approached by someone who makes it very clear to you that they want your attention. That they want your help."

"Oh, that," I said, cupping my hands around the candle. "The thing is, Mom, that's actually already happened."

We stayed up so late talking Friday night that I was like a zombie the next day. I had planned to go to the library, which the school kept open one Saturday morning a month for the studious and the procrastinating. Jac had a "cello lesson" in the late morning (I was starting to think of everything relating to her ball and chain as surrounded by quotes now), and since we'd never actually made any headway on the bio project, Saturday morning seemed like a good time to get some research out of the way. I walked to school, partly to clear my fuzzy head and partly because my mother had scheduled a session, and I didn't want to ask her for a ride. It was bleak and the kind of drizzle had started that looked like it was going to change into a downpour at any second. This was the kind of day a girl should stay in bed reading the latest *Gossip Girl* book, or park in the papa-san chair in front of the television for the *Psychic Pet Detective* marathon. But to be honest, after the hours of conversation with my mother about everything from spontaneous spirit channeling to the theory of demonic possession, I really needed to get away from the house for a little while.

I saw this show once about rich girls and their lavish sweet-sixteen parties, and they showed this one girl who had lived in poverty and pretty grim circumstances until these super-billionaires came and adopted her when she was fifteen. Then, literally overnight, she was living in a mansion with unlimited cash at her disposal. By the time they filmed the show, her eleven-month transformation had left her unrecognizable. She'd had a Japanese hair straightening treatment and highlights that cost more than most of us pay for two months of summer camp (I know this because she announced the cost of everything to the camera). She wore Stella McCartney skinny jeans and a Michael Kors top over an eight-hundred-dollar pair of cowboy boots, which she claimed she would probably only wear once before throwing out. And fashion modifications aside, the girl had developed a major attitude, nastily cutting down girls with less money or prettier faces than she had, happily insulting and trashing them right on camera. And I watched her and remembered wondering where the other version of her had gone — the version of the girl who'd spent her first fifteen years stamping on cockroaches in the kitchen every morning and wearing Faded Glory jeans she'd got on final clearance sale at Wal-Mart. And the scary thing was, the old version of the girl seemed completely gone. It was like the minute she got rich, she transformed into a viperous creature with an unlimited hunger for designer clothing, world-class spa treatments, and a desire to ruin the lives of other girls.

Okay, try to stay with me here. Maybe it's like comparing apples and . . . Twinkies, but I was afraid something along these lines might happen to me. I was afraid that becoming a medium basically overnight was going to wipe the old me clean out of reality and replace me with something . . .

less normal. Different. And though I'd given up hopes of being welcomed at the cool table and enjoying a Quinn Irvin-esque level of general popularity, I still entertained this wild dream that I could somehow get by without turning into a giant, séance-throwing freak.

The school library looked gray and institutional under the dark skies. It resembled a low-security jail, which seemed somehow symbolic. Like we were all prisoners in school. And the wardens were our teachers.

But it was too early in the morning to be getting deep. I shook off the thoughts and went inside. The library was pretty empty. There were two guys from Computer Club bent over one of the library's computer terminals. You could never tell if those guys were doing cutting edge research, playing Tomb Raider, or trying to hack into the grading system. They didn't seem to notice me come in, and that was fine. I preferred to remain anonymous.

I went to the back of the library, to the table where Jac and I had experienced our little supernatural phenomena. I really only went back there because it was secluded. Even there, I wasn't quite alone. I could hear a girl's voice through the stacks, talking either to someone who was given no opportunity to interrupt, or on a cell phone. She spoke in the MTV dialect, making her voice sound scratchy and drawing out her vowels for an eternity before ending her sentences in a question.

"So I went the whole week, that's like *seven* days, totally sticking to the South Beach diet, like, to the *letter*, right? And after seven days,

I lost *one* pound? And then on Sunday my mother shows up with this cheesecake? And I ate, like, two pieces? So the next day, I've gained *two pounds!* So it's, like, what? If I ever go off this diet for, like, one minute, I'll automatically gain back *twice* what it took me a week to lose? Because I'm sorry, but, like, if the whole world expects us to be thin, they need to make the government issue personal trainers for free to taxpayers or whatever?"

I sat frozen, unable to stop eavesdropping, unsure if what I was hearing signaled the demise of Western civilization or was just hysterically funny.

"My 'rents are going to have to get me lipo," the voice continued drawling. "I don't care how old you have to be. I'll get a fake ID? 'Cause right now I have to wear this Lycra tummy flattener just to get into these jeans, or whatever, and it's, like, cutting into my skin?"

Why were girls like Brooklyn so obsessed with what they weighed? I didn't have anything even close to resembling a flat stomach, and I probably never would. I might obsess about seeing dead people and being a freak at school, but even I realize these are problems a Lycra girdle isn't going to fix.

"Being fat is for losers and the, like, underprivileged people who don't belong to a gym, or whatever. It's, like, when we get into college the right people are not going to want to hang with us unless we're size six or below, okay? My parents may be morons, but they should totally understand that. They, like, forcibly woke me and dragged me to the library this morning, as if they can actually make me study because this paper is, like, half my final grade. I'm getting all that bio stuff off the Internet anyway, for, like, fifty bucks. Completely written."

Strike that. Replace it with "the decline of Western civilization."

"Hello? Can you hear me? Can you hear me now? Hello?"

I heard the unmistakable sound of a cell phone being snapped shut. Before I had a chance to think, a chair scraped against the floor, and the kind of footsteps made by expensive leather high-heeled boots exploded like gunfire.

Someone was walking briskly past my table — a blur with a Chanel bag. But then she froze and looked over her shoulder directly at me.

It was Brooklyn Bigelow.

An expression of acute embarrassment and horror crossed her face as she realized I might have been listening to her very personal cell phone conversation, which, of course, I had. A few seconds later the expression of embarrassment was replaced by a look of sheer contempt.

"Ugh!" she said, tossing her hair. I realize I don't get out all that much, but Brooklyn was the first person I'd ever seen actually toss her hair. "Where do you get your clothes — a thrift store? You look like you work at McDonald's."

I probably should have pretended I hadn't heard. That would have been the safest thing to do. But Brooklyn looked so sour and patronizing, her lips scrunched into such a tiny mean line, I just couldn't sit there passively.

"Well, you obviously have special needs that a thrift store just can't meet, Brooklyn, what with your Lycra girdle issues."

Brooklyn's mouth dropped open in astonishment and she blushed. Then she closed her mouth and narrowed her eyes.

"You might want to check them out yourself. Looks like you need one worse than I do. Actually, I almost feel sorry for you, Kat. From what I hear, you might as well have been raised in a cult. See, I know all about your weirdo *mother* now."

I stared impassively at Brooklyn. What was this girl even doing in a library in the first place? She should have been turned away at the door as underqualified.

"She's supposedly a medium? Please! Everyone knows from *Myth Busters* all that stuff is a load of garbage. She's a con artist. It's disgusting, and it totally goes against the Bible."

"What goes against the Bible, Brooklyn?" I asked, feeling a wave of rage rise into my throat.

"Séances and Ouija boards and pretending you have fake powers to get money from people! That's, like, totally against the Bible, and everyone knows it."

"Yeah? Which part of the Bible says that?" I demanded.

Brooklyn made a little explosive sound of impatience.

"Like, the entire thing?" she exclaimed piously. "Like, not watching false American idols, or whatever?"

Oh, man. If she wasn't so vile that would really have been very funny.

"You don't fit in here, and you never will," Brooklyn said. "No one likes you but that stupid cello girl. No one wants to hang out with you. You're a joke in this school. You should just move, or transfer to some hippie granola school that takes welfare cases."

"And miss welcoming you back to school after your first lipo treatment? I just couldn't."

Brooklyn's face was taking on a purple tint. Her hands were on her hips, and she seemed to be trembling.

"I'm going to make it my personal business to make sure everyone in this school knows that your mother is nothing but a con-artist," Brooklyn hissed. "Because when people know the truth, it won't be enough for them to just not hang out with you. They're not going to tolerate you staying at this school. None of us will. You'll be a total outcast, and your mother will be the laughingstock of the county."

And that, as they say, was the straw that broke the camel's back. I shouldn't have done it, but I think you might understand why I did.

First, I stood up, for effect. I don't really know why I thought it would help. I think it was something I saw on an old episode of *Bewitched.* Then I stared at Brooklyn for a long moment, narrowing my eyes to mimic hers.

"You seem awfully sure that my mother is a fake, Brooklyn. It's pretty interesting that no scientific research has ever been able to prove the supernatural does *not* exist, and yet you seem really confident that it doesn't. You better be right, Brooklyn. Because what if you're not? What if my mother really *does* have the ability to interact with spirits? Is that really the kind of person you want to be messing with? And what about me? Can you be sure I didn't inherit a supernatural gift myself? Because guess what, Brooklyn? I *have.* The powers my mother has are very real, and I have them, too. Do you want to test me? Do you want to take the two percent risk that I can do what I say I can do? Because I *can*, Brooklyn. I can conjure up a spirit right here. I can even arrange for something nice and ugly and demonic to start haunting you. All you have to do is stand right here while I run through the incantation. Want to try? Want to see? It might prove to be fake, just like you said. Or you might end up in a whole lot of trouble. Once you mess with the dead, no plastic surgeon is going to be able to fix you."

Time for a dramatic pause. I watched Brooklyn's expression, a little worried that she might just burst out laughing. But no, Brooklyn had a nervous expression creeping onto her face. I continued to recite my work of almost pure fiction.

"All I need to do is chant a simple little

incantation. It's so simple, Brooklyn, if you have the gift like I do. Now just stand still, and I'll get started."

I raised both hands above my head and closed my eyes. Then I began to rock slowly back and forth.

"Cassiel, Galadriel, Zarathustra, Oberon. I call to the four corners of the earth, O spirits. Arise. . . . I summon thee. Ariiiiiise. . . ."

"Stop it," Brooklyn hissed. "Stop it!!"

I opened one eye halfway and peered at her. She was clutching her Chanel bag to her chest as if it were a baby. She was taking small, tentative steps backward.

"Arise, ye spirits. O elemental ones, I invoke thee. In the name of fire, earth, air, and water. Ariiiiiiiiiiiiiise . . . ," I intoned again.

Brooklyn took a final step back and collided with a magazine stack. This seemed to bring her pretty much to the end of her rope. She let out a piercing scream, smacked at the magazine rack as if it were an attacking rodent, and hightailed it out of the library, slamming the door behind her.

I sank back into my chair, laughing silently. I felt guilty about what I'd just done, but Brooklyn was awful! She deserved to have the designer boot-cut pants scared off of her. And the look on her face when I'd started chanting .. it was priceless. I didn't know how I could ever do it justice when I described it to Jac. I made a quiet little chuckle, then sighed deeply. As I breathed, I felt something nudging at my consciousness. Just a something. I wasn't at all sure what. I opened my eyes.

Suzanne Bennis stood in front of me, looking directly into my eyes.

I jumped involuntarily, startled. Suzanne

didn't move. It was as if she'd been standing there for a very long time. Waiting.

It seemed she could see me, yet there was no expression at all on her face. She looked completely devoid of all emotion. Robotic. I felt a little shiver down my spine. And though I'd seen her here before, though I felt certain she haunted this room, it occurred to me that this time she might have come in response to my summons. My fake, bust-Brooklyn-Bigelow's-chops summons.

I had somehow been able to send Suzanne away before. I had somehow been able to communicate to her that I wasn't ready to interact with her. And now, although more or less by accident, I might have called her up. This was my fault, and now I had better do something. I have to make it up as I went along.

"Suzanne?" I said.

Something sparked in her eyes, but she said nothing. She looked exactly the same as she had when I saw her with Shoshanna, and as she had in the yearbook. Same worn gray clothing. Same hollow cheeks. Same fat white-blond braids.

"Suzanne," I repeated. "Suzanne Bennis."

Something gleamed in her hand. I glanced down and saw that she was holding a flute. She continued to stare at me impassively.

What was I supposed to do? God, I had spent all that time talking to my mother about the spirits. Why hadn't I asked her that simple question? What did Suzanne Bennis want from me?

"My name is Kat," I said. "I can see you, Suzanne."

No response. Duh. She knew I could see her. I wasn't going about this the right way at all. I didn't have a clue. I didn't belong here — I belonged in remedial medium school.

Then Suzanne took a step toward me. It took every ounce of self-control I had not to slide my chair backward to restore the space between us. She placed one hand on the table and leaned toward me, her braids swinging forward. Her hands looked flat and two-dimensional, like I was seeing them on television. Her voice, when it came, was barely above a whisper.

"I know," she said.

"You know what?" I whispered back.

"I already know," she said. "That I'm dead."

And she blinked out of sight again, the space where she'd been filled with the sudden loud clanging of the school fire alarm.

Chapter 11

So much for my Saturday. I had to wait in the library for an hour with the two Computer Club guys before security could determine that the alarm was triggered by someone opening the fire door that led directly outside. It wasn't too much of a stretch for me to figure out who had been in such a hurry to get out of the building that they'd tripped the alarm. But I didn't rat Brooklyn out to security. It wasn't worth the bother, and I didn't want to implicate myself as the cause of her hasty exit. I was getting pretty anxious to get out of the library myself.

Suzanne hadn't come back. But I was growing increasingly uncomfortable, and I suspected it had more to do with the prank I'd pulled on Brooklyn than with Suzanne's appearance. In my heart I knew that I'd misused my powers and that I was in danger of crossing some kind of line. I tried to put the thought out of my mind. It was a stupid trick, yes, but a small one. It was over now. No real harm done.

But I certainly had neither the energy nor the inclination to stay in the library working on my bio project. What I wanted now was to get out of the library and talk to Jac.

Outside, the rain had held off but the sky was still iron gray. I began to walk toward the street where Jac lived. I'd never been to her apartment, but I knew which building it was in. Since I didn't have a phone, I decided just to show up unannounced. There was always a certain amount of risk involved in an unplanned stop-by, but I had to see Jac. And secretly, I was a little curious about her home life, which she didn't discuss much. I knew that her mother was obsessed with Jac's cello playing and that her father was some kind of computer genius who tested software programs and wasn't around much. That was pretty much all I knew, though.

The apartment complex was a plain redbrick building of about five stories. I checked the buzzers at the front door and found the right one, a ground-floor apartment. I rang the buzzer and waited, pressing my hands against my stomach to quiet the butterflies that were spastically flapping around my intestines.

After a few moments, the apartment door opened and a woman who had to be Jac's mother stood and regarded me. I gave her my politest Miss Manners smile and extended my hand.

"Hello. You must be Jac's mom. I'm her friend Kat, from school."

For a minute, the woman didn't say anything and I was afraid Jac had never said anything about me. Or worse, that I'd come to the wrong apartment. But then the woman smiled, or at least her mouth did. Her eyes remained the same — cool and appraising.

"Of course, Kat. How nice to meet you. I don't think we were expecting you?"

"No, I'm sorry. I mean, I was just in the neighborhood, and I . . . thought I'd drop by."

Okay, that was lame.

"Well, why don't you have a seat in the living room and I'll get Jac. Since you're here now."

How heartwarming. I tried to smile again, but it was hard in the face of such a cold front. Jac's mother had the same features and coloring as she did, the red hair and the small, pointy face. But where Jac's face was open and friendly, this woman seemed closed and steely. I could certainly see where Jac came by her fashion sense, if it was her choice at all. Her mother was wearing a pink-and-white floral linen shirt, pink twill pants, and white suede loafers. Her red hair was pulled back by one of those wide, expensive looking headbands, and a set of perfect pearl earrings dangled from her ears. All this for a rainy Saturday around the house. Back at home, my mother was probably wearing faded black sweatpants and an oversized Grateful Dead concert T-shirt from the mid-seventies.

I sat on an uncomfortable-looking chair in the living room and peered cautiously around. The room looked like a museum for untouched upholstery and highly polished furniture. On a table near the window I noticed a number of framed photographs, and I got up to take a closer look at them.

They were all of Jac playing the cello — every single one. In some she looked like she couldn't be more than four or five years old, her little arms wrapped around the enormous instrument, her forehead wrinkled in concentration. In a few she was standing with other musicians, each balancing a cello in front of them, her tiny one next to the bigger adult versions. In another, Jac seemed to be winning some kind of award. There must have been fifteen photographs here, each framed in ornate silver, and yet in not one of them was Jac smiling. A girl didn't need to summon Sigmund Freud back from the grave to figure out that this little musician was not a happy camper.

I heard someone come into the room and I turned, expecting to greet Jac. Instead, I saw a small, wizened old man with bright, twinkling eyes and a slight, stooped figure. He was dressed in a forest green cardigan and old but well-preserved tweed pants. He smiled and nodded at me, and I got a sudden, warm whiff of pipe tobacco. As I looked at him, I noticed a flatness to his outline and felt a buzz of energy in the air.

He's dead, I thought suddenly.

Now, here's the really nutso part. It occurred to me that this was a person I wanted to be around. His manner was so welcoming, his aura so intelligent and joyful, I just wanted to hear his voice and maybe to make him laugh. Maybe I was way overdue for a trip to the funny farm, but I really felt this was the loveliest dead person I'd ever come across. I smiled back at him, and he gave me another little grandfatherly nod, his eyes dancing.

"Kat!"

The floor seemed to shift a little, like an elevator that's not quite running smoothly. Jac was standing in the doorway of the living room. She cast a quick glance over her shoulder, then came into the room, walking right through the place the little old man had been standing five seconds earlier.

"What are you doing here?"

"Aren't you glad to see me?" I asked.

Jac grabbed my upper arms and squeezed them.

"You have no idea how glad I am to see

you. But," she said leaning forward, lowering her voice to a whisper, "my mom gets all stressed out when people show up unannounced. Let's go to my room."

Jac led me silently out of the living room and down a hallway, decorated with large prints of birds, each spaced precisely the same distance one from the next, eight to each wall. Everything looked so highly dusted and perfect I was afraid to breathe. I tiptoed behind Jac, who led me to a door at the end of the hallway. I followed my friend meekly into her room.

Like the rest of the apartment, Jac's room had a highly decorated feel, but it was also strewn with clues to Jac's real personality. On the bed lay an open copy of a glossy tabloid magazine featuring a spread on the latest marriage of Tori Spelling and a series of speculative before and after photographs comparing her various features and theorizing which ones had been surgically enhanced.

"Jac, you have *Star* magazine, you delinquent!" I cried gleefully.

Jac shushed me and shut the door.

"Woman, shut your mouth," she hissed. "My mother will have to be surgically peeled off the ceiling if she finds me reading that."

I started to laugh, but I could see from Jac's face that she wasn't really joking.

"God," I said. "That's . . . harsh."

"She doesn't deliberately try to be harsh," Jac explained, plopping down on the bed and patting a spot for me to plop down next to her. "But let's just say that in the dictionary, next to the entry for *generation gap*, is a full-color photo of my mother."

"Wow. I wonder what entry my mother's photo is next to?" I asked.

Jac grinned.

"So what's up? I thought you were going to slave away on your bio thing today."

I sighed.

"I was. I will. I actually went to the library this morning. And listen to what happened."

I gave Jac a thorough account of my library experiences, both natural and supernatural. She listened without interrupting me, her eyes growing particularly wide at the detail of Suzanne Bennis holding a flute in her hand.

"How did she look?" Jac asked eagerly.

"Well, you know, Jac. Not all that great. Aside from the fact that she's been dead for, like, forty years. Her face is kind of hollow, you know? Like she's exhausted, or sick, or not sleeping. And she was wearing the same thing again, from the picture. This kind of ratty gray outfit. Either she wore it all the time, or there is one particular moment that her spirit is stuck in, I'm not sure."

"Okay. And after she was gone?"

"Nothing else important happened. Security switched the fire alarm off. I had to hang out forever while they made sure there was no real fire or anything. As soon as they said I could go, I hightailed it right here."

Jac looked thoughtful.

"And you're sure she disappeared before the fire alarm went off, or did it happen the other way around?" she asked.

"No, it was before. I was looking right at her, and *boom!* She was just gone. Then the alarm went."

"So whatever she wanted to say, she was done saying it?"

"That's right," I replied. "The thing I'm confused about, though, is whether she would have appeared to me, anyway."

"What do you mean?"

I sighed.

"Like I said, I was doing this thing, you know. To freak Brooklyn out."

"Your Voodoo Mama bit," Jac described helpfully.

"Yeah, okay. I know it sounds ridiculous. But you should have seen her face, Jac. She went from, like, designer witch to basket case in five seconds."

"But then Suzanne came, and you're saying you don't know if she was trying to contact you again, or if she came because she thought you were calling for her."

I nodded.

"In a nutshell, yes," I said.

"Do you know what I think we need?" Jac asking, sitting up and swinging her feet to the floor.

"Our own reality show?"

Jac winced.

"Don't even go there," she said. "If my mother knew there was such a thing as reality shows, I'm sure she'd be peddling *Stifled Junior Cellist* to every station in the country. No, what we need is more information."

Jac went over to her desk and flipped open a laptop, powering it up and sitting down in the chair.

"What are you doing?"

"Come here," Jac said.

The familiar symbol of AOL flickered on-screen. Jac typed something deftly.

"What's your password?"

"Barley," Jac replied, sitting back to wait for an Internet connection.

"Barley? Like Barleycorn?"

"Barley like Matthew Barley," Jac said, pointing to a picture hanging near the door.

It was a black-and-white photograph of what looked to be the world's cutest boy, holding a cello.

"Classical music's studliest cellist," Jac explained. "I've got two of his CDs. Okay, here we go. Google away."

I got up off the bed and pulled up a little stool next to Jac's chair.

"What are you Googling?"

"Our school," Jac replied. "Bet you anything there's a site with all sorts of stuff."

And sure enough, there it was. A recent photograph of our school, with the outline of the school seal superimposed on the picture. There were sections for student life, faculty, courses, sports, and history. The main screen had a montage of recent candid shots of students looking robust and happy. Predictably, Shoshanna appeared in two of them, surrounded by admirers.

We both leaned closer to the screen, reading the headings.

"I don't see a section for *unexplained hauntings* here," said Jac.

"Very funny," I said, getting up and going to examine the photograph of Matthew Barley more closely. He was hot.

"Wait," Jac exclaimed. "Hey, now, *here's* something!"

"What?"

"There's something here about how our school is the longest continuingly operating educational facility in the county."

I rolled my eyes.

"Gosh, Jac, that's like, revolutionary."

"No, shut up and listen, Voodoo Mama. It says the school was established at this same location in eighteen twenty, and only closed its doors once, for three weeks in nineteen sixty, when a meningitis epidemic spread through the area."

"Nineteen sixty? Isn't that the year Suzanne died?"

Jac nodded, still staring at the screen. She scrolled down a few times.

"I'm going to try putting her name in the search field. Maybe they mention her because, you know, she died and everything."

I reluctantly left Matthew Barley on the wall and joined Jac at the computer.

"Nope," I said as the search field indicated there was no match to the name Bennis. "I guess that would have been too easy."

"And I guess they're not going to want to put stuff like that on the Web site, even if it did happen half a lifetime ago. People don't want to know that students in their school can die."

"But if we think it was that meningitis epidemic, it's not like it's anybody's fault, right? I mean, back in those days there were all sorts of infectious diseases that kids actually died of. Did you ever read *Little Women?*" I asked.

"Oh, I hated reading that book," Jac said. "Because I knew when I started that one of the sisters was going to die, and it was, like, why am I putting myself through this?"

"I know," I said. I had felt exactly the same way.

"There's really not much useful information on this Web site, other than the thing about the epidemic," Jac said, still scrolling down the screens. "It does say there's an extensive archive of the school's history in the library files in the subbasement. I guess we should look there."

"Great! Because the only thing more fun

than a haunted library is the dark subbasement *under* the haunted library, right?"

Jac shrugged. Then I heard her mother's voice calling her, and Jac winced at the sound.

The door to her room opened, and her mother peered inside, looking like the poster child for free-floating anxiety disorder.

"Jackie, didn't you hear me calling you?"

"No, we —"

"I'm sure you simply aren't aware of the time. You have a lesson in forty minutes, and I haven't even heard you tune your cello. Miss Wittencourt's time is very, very important, Jackie. Why I need to tell you what you already know is beyond me."

I got up quickly. I wanted to say that Jac didn't like being called Jackie, but then I guessed her mom would already know that.

"I was just going," I said. Neither mother nor daughter seemed to hear me.

"Mother," Jac said suddenly, "just give me a minute, okay? I have *company*. God!"

Jac's mother breathed tensely in and out through her nose a few times, her lips pressed tightly together. Then she turned and left the room.

Jac groaned.

"Sorry."

"It's okay. Walk me to the door?"

Jac complied, linking her arm through mine and escorting me down the bird-festooned hallway to the front door. Her mother was nowhere in sight.

"I'll call you," she said.

"Not if I call you first," I countered. "Oh, and Jac?" I whispered, just before I slipped out the door.

"Yeah?"

"Your apartment is haunted."

Chapter 12

The thing with the fake incantation to scare Brooklyn was kind of pressing on me. So when my mom made me banana pancakes and soy sausage patties for Sunday brunch, I decided to bring it up. Hypothetically, of course.

"So, Mom?"

She was standing in a faded purple kimono by the table, parceling out soy sausage patties to each of our plates. She gave me a wide, bright-eyed smile.

"I have a question. Hypothetical, of course."

"Of course," my mother repeated, putting my plate in front of me and pulling up a chair for herself.

"Be careful of the syrup — it's hot," she warned.

"Okay," I said, pouring way more than I needed over my pancakes and sausage both.

"So, let's just say, you know, for the heck of it, that I'm dealing with this person or people who are small-minded in the worst possible way. You know, your basic haters. And it's the usual drill — they have more money than God and wear most of it every day and seek out less wealthy life-forms to torture, humiliate, and ostracize."

"Sounds very familiar so far," my mother said, spreading some yogurt-based butter on a wheat-free eggless bagel. "Sounds like a conversation that could be happening in any state across the country at this very moment."

"Yep. Except there's a wrinkle. A kind of unusual complication. See, in addition to being a regulation hater, this girl is also a member of the Moral Moron Society."

"The Moral Moron Society?" my mom asked, taking a long sip of her steaming Lapsang souchong tea. "I'm not sure I'm familiar with them."

"That's because I just officially named the group yesterday," I said. "So, actually, hypothetically, of course —"

"Of course," my mother interrupted with a small smile.

"Of course, you could say she's a founding member of the Moral Moron Society. And what this society does is, it checks around its immediate environment for anything that doesn't operate within the confines of the accepted social traditions of this country."

"Ah, the Spanish Inquisition. Nobody expects it," my mother said, still smiling as she warmed her hands on her teacup.

"You're on the right track, but you're a few centuries too late. I'm talking —"

"Hypothetically, of course," she interjected.

"— of course, about present-day. To be more specific, about yesterday. So when someone in this society thinks they've hit on someone whose behavior is at odds with traditional rules, they kind of go on the offensive."

"Which involves..." my mother helpfully prompted.

"Which involves their using words like *witch* and *con artist,* and making threats of exposure followed by social shunning. Oh, and a strong suggestion that this person should transfer to a different school, one that takes, how did she put it, 'hippie welfare cases.'"

"Yikes," my mother said, putting her teacup down. "Kat, tell me someone didn't actually say things like that to you."

"Continuing hypothetically," I went on, "let's say that this person's temper got the better of her, and she decided to have a little fun. Since the pot had already called the kettle black, you know. So she sort of performed this fake incantation to raise the dead. Just to kind of freak the hater out."

"And the result was?"

"Significant freakage to an amusing and satisfying degree, followed by a rapid exit through an alarmed fire door."

My mother sat back in her chair, looking thoughtful and mildly amused.

"Well, Kat, since this hypothetical hater used the word *con artist*, I'm presuming she was accusing either you or me of faking our ability to interact with the dead."

I nodded, deciding now was as good a time as any to drop the hypothetical aspect of the story and accept that the identity of the witch and con artist had never been in doubt. My mother probably already had a clearer sense of what had gone on in the library than I did, and she hadn't even been there.

"When someone accuses you of lying about something this central to who you are, that's an attack. And the fact that you made her fearful shows you that in her heart she does believe such abilities exist, and she's afraid of them. She was wrong to come at you the way she did, Kat. No doubt about it. But be very careful before you set a precedent in how you use your gift. If it becomes a weapon for you, even an unintentional one, you'll find yourself on a very complicated path.

"Everything has two sides, Kat, including what we do. All of our myths reflect that. For every aspect of light there is an equal one of dark. For every force of good, there is a countering force of evil. Jedi versus Sith, to put it in movie terms. The principle of opposing forces does spring from a basic and very ancient truth. But to use your powers to threaten or intimidate someone, even if it seems like a joke, is still an act that mixes dark energy with light energy. You need to stay with the light energy completely, Kat. The only rule of using your gift is that you always use it with the intention to *help*. And when the Moral Morons come calling, well, you're going to have to find a way to thicken your skin."

"You would have taken the high road, right?" I asked, pouring even more syrup onto my plate and creating an ocean of sugary liquid surrounding my pancake islands. "You would have just let her call you a witch and a con artist, and you wouldn't have felt the need to prove anything to her."

My mother shrugged.

"Having come face-to-face with plenty of charter members of the Moral Moron Society, I know how angry and sick you must have felt. And I don't believe any real harm was done this time. But at the same time, you took her negative energy, and you engaged it. You fed back into her dark energy, instead of responding with light."

I wasn't sure I understood what that meant, but it definitely wasn't a compliment on how I'd handled things. I sort of wished we could go back to things being hypothetical for the next part, but there's never any going back.

"The thing is, Mom, after Broo — after the Moral Moron took off, it seems my spirit summons had a very real effect. Because Suzanne Bennis, the girl from the sixties that I told you about, she suddenly manifested. Like, less than a minute after my fake summons."

My mother put her teacup down and gave me an appraising look.

"You mean you think you might have called this spirit up accidentally?" she asked.

I nodded, glumly.

"Did she do or say anything when she apparated?"

I closed my eyes, trying to see it in my mind's eye.

"She — she definitely saw me. She was standing there looking at me. Then she leaned over and put her hands on the table where I was sitting. I wasn't sure what I was supposed to be doing, or what she expected of me. That's the one thing you and I really didn't go over when we talked about it the other night. So I just kind of said her name, you know, to show I knew it. And I said my name. Oh, and I told her I could see her."

My mother nodded, her head cocked slightly to one side. Max, lying at her feet, raised his enormous head and watched her.

"And then I just introduced myself. And she said . . ."

"She spoke?" my mother interrupted, looking surprised.

I nodded. "Is that unusual?"

"It can be. Creating physical speech requires the control of a great deal of energy, energy a spirit is already using to appear physical. Usually the communication takes place on a mental level first. Like telepathy.

You get images, scenes. Maybe the odd word or two. But it's very hard, unless there is an existing source of energy already there to tap into. What did she say?"

"Here's where it gets a little weirder. I said something like, 'What do you mean, you know?' And she looks right at me, and she says, 'I already know that I'm dead.' And then she just disappeared in an instant. So now I have no idea what happened. I mean, did she come because she thought I was summoning her and leave because it was obvious I hadn't? Or would she have come anyway when she sensed me in the library? Do you think I've messed this up somehow because I used my powers to play a joke?"

My mother shook her head, sliding a soy sausage around her plate like it was a hockey puck.

"I don't think so, Kat. I'm just going on instinct here. But my guess is Suzanne sensed you were in the physical realm she inhabits, and she manifested because of that. You didn't call her up the first time, after all. She sought you out. Something attracted her to you. I'd also guess that when Suzanne told you she realizes she is dead, she was indicating that she doesn't need your help in guiding her over to the next world. If she knows she's dead, then she is staying in this world by choice, not through disorientation."

"Which means . . ."

"Which means whatever help she needs is about something entirely different. And the only way to find out what that could be is to have a meaningful contact with her in a safe setting where time is not a factor and where you won't run the risk of someone from the Moral Moron Society or any other group blundering onto you."

"So you're saying . . ."

"I'm saying," my mother said, finishing her tea with a big gulp, "that you need to have a séance."

Jac wasn't home when I called the next day, and I waited impatiently by the phone, wondering where she would have gone on a Sunday afternoon. My mother and I had talked late into the night, and now that I knew what I had to do, I wanted it done. I wanted Jac to help me search through the school's archives during lunch period on Monday so that we had all the information we needed before moving forward with an actual séance. I felt an unpleasant weight of anticipation, like when you know you have a doctor's appointment that's going to involve a shot.

Jac finally called just before dinner. My mother was putting the final touches on her signature hummus and wheatgrass tacos (don't judge if you haven't tasted), but when the phone rang, my mother communicated her basic don't worry about the food, it won't go bad sentiment.

"I was beginning to think your mother hadn't given you my phone message," I said as soon as I got on the phone.

"No, she wouldn't do that," Jac replied. "She can be as manipulative as all get out with concert bookers, but she's never really tried to mess with my personal life. Which doesn't say much, actually, because until I met you I pretty much had no personal life whatsoever."

"I'm honored," I said, and I meant it.

"Likewise," Jac said.

"So how did the cello lesson go yesterday?"

"That's the thing, Kat. You won't believe this — it was *amazing!*"

"Really? Did you play?"

"Nope. Not so much as a note. No, Jac, I was sitting with Miss Wittencourt and my cello, doing nothing as usual. Except I'd stopped at Dunkin' Donuts on the way and gotten a bladder buster — one of those sixteen-ounce iced coffees — which I pretty much drank in one sip. So about forty minutes into the lesson I had to go really really badly."

"Okay," I said, thinking this didn't sound like something I'd attach an adjective like *amazing* to.

"Because the thing is, I'd never been to the bathroom at Miss Wittencourt's before," Jac said.

"Oh, right!" I said, though I had absolutely no idea where Jac was going with this.

"So there's all these pictures hanging in the hallway," Jac continued. "It was kind of dimly lit, you know, but I had time to kill. So after using the bathroom I sort of stood around, waiting for my eyes to adjust to the light. And once they did, I could see the pictures."

"Were they naughty?" I asked, getting a sudden humorous flash of Miss Wittencourt as a reformed pinup girl.

"Ew, no," Jac replied, sounding indignant. "No, listen to this. Kat, there were pictures of musicians. From recent ones to a really long time ago. And I was looking at some of the older ones, and I start seeing pictures of a kind of very familiar face playing the flute!"

"You don't mean Suzanne Bennis?"

"Exactly. There were, like, four or five pictures of her. And that wasn't all. There were also pictures of Miss Wittencourt and Suzanne playing *together.*"

"But Suzanne died almost fifty years ago! It's impossible, Jac," I cried, wishing at the same time that it wasn't impossible — that Miss Wittencourt was a real live link to Suzanne.

"But it *is* possible, oh, ye of no mathematical aptitude," Jac countered.

"Repeat, please?"

"Let's say Miss Wittencourt was in her late twenties the year Suzanne died. Give or take a few years. That would make her in her mid-seventies today. News flash, Voodoo Mama. People do live that long. Anyway, we don't need math, because I went back to see Miss Wittencourt today. She was pretty surprised to see me without my cello, but she asked me in and she made me some lemonade. After a while, I finally worked up the nerve, and I just came right out and *asked* her about the pictures. I told her I'd seen Suzanne's picture in an old yearbook and recognized her as the same girl in the pictures Miss Wittencourt had. And I sort of prodded her to tell me about it. And you're not going to believe what I found out."

My mind reeled as I tried to guess.

"Kat, are you there?"

"I'm here," I said. "I'm updating my brain."

"Miss Wittencourt was Suzanne Bennis's flute teacher," Jac stated. "At our school."

"But she teaches cello," I said. "In, like, this decade."

"She teaches everything, and apparently she has for ages," Jac said. "I know she also teaches violin, and apparently the flute, too. And I told you she used to be this virtuoso cellist herself. She gave some big-time concerts way back then. Anyway, she said Suzanne was one of the most gifted flutists she had ever heard. So I asked her what had happened to Suzanne. And she didn't say anything for a long time, and I thought maybe I'd asked too much. But then she said Suzanne had gotten very sick and died, and what a terrible blow it had been. And she said something else, too — that there was suddenly nothing left of Suzanne but a scholarship in her name."

"A music scholarship?"

"Yep," Jac said. "One I've never heard a thing about, which is sort of hard to believe when you consider that my mother re-searched the music program at school like her life depended on it. She knows about every prize and competition within a fifty-mile radius. I can't understand why she wouldn't have found out about a scholarship at the very school she was moving me to."

"Okay, let's think this through," I said. My stomach was beginning to rumble, but now was not the time to be thinking about lunch. "Miss Wittencourt was Suzanne's teacher. Then Suzanne got sick, probably of meningitis. Suzanne was a seriously talented musician, according to Miss Wittencourt, who would know. And there was some kind of scholarship started after Suzanne died. But how does any of this explain why Suzanne is still hanging around school more than forty years after the rest of her class graduated?"

"Hey, I'm just a former cello prodigy. You're the medium."

"Thanks, Jac, for the reality check."

"Did you talk to your mom about it?" she asked.

"Yeah, actually I did."

"And?"

"And she said I needed to . . . you know."

"Do I? Pretend I don't," Jac said.

"To have a kind of séance. To prepare myself with everything I can find out about Suzanne and then have an organized attempt at communication. And she said the best time to do it is just before dawn, because that's when the veil between the two worlds is often the thinnest."

"Wowzers."

"Exactly. And the thing is, I don't know how I'm going to do that."

"Make it up as you go," Jac suggested helpfully.

"Funny. But I'm not talking about just the séance. I'm talking about how I could possibly get into the library before dawn. It's open after school, but only till six. It's open one Saturday a month, but not until eight in the morning. What am I supposed to do, break into the place?"

"Well, yeah, you could," Jac said, sounding very cheerful for someone suggesting that her one and only friend commit what is probably a felony in this state. "Or, you could find a person of your acquaintance, someone, say, inclined to do you a favor, who for very complicated reasons partially involving the lack of soundproofing in apartment buildings constructed after the early 1970s has a special arrangement with the school authorities to enter the music wing in the very early morning hours so that she can sit and stare at her cello without disturbing the peace of anyone in the vicinity. Through a door that also happens to give access to the library."

"You have a key? You have a key to get into the school?" I cried.

"That's more or less the concise version of what I just said, yes."

"When can you use it?"

"They never really said when I could or couldn't use it. It's for cello practicing."

"Will you help me? Will you get me in and help me with the séance?"

"I'll try," Jac replied. "I can't promise I won't pull a Brooklyn and bolt. But I'll try. As long as there are no bugs involved."

"I want to do it as soon as possible," I said firmly. "It's hard to explain, Jac, but I feel like Suzanne is kind of pressing on me. I've got to take the next step, and I can't put it off. But my mother said I need to make sure I have every bit of information about Suzanne that I can gather, to help me find out what might be binding Suzanne to the school. The only place I can think of that might have that information is the historical archives you read about on the Web site. If we skip lunch tomorrow, we could go down and look through the files. We might find something that will help. Then we could have the séance Tuesday morning, if you can really get us in at dawn."

"Does it all have to happen so fast?" Jac asked.

"Yes," I said firmly. "Suzanne knows I can see her, and she's already appeared to me three times at school. The whole thing is stressing me out, Jac. Seriously, you cannot imagine. I'm not *used* to this stuff. I need to find out what's keeping Suzanne here and give her the help she needs so things can get back to normal. I've barely done *anything* on that bio project. It's bad enough that I'm seeing ghosts. I don't need to get put on academic probation on top of that."

Jac sighed.

"I guess we'll be skipping lunch tomorrow, then."

I could have kissed her right through the phone.

The librarian looked surprised that we wanted to visit the archives, like she got such a request only once in a blue moon. But she didn't ask any questions — she just had us sign a list and then gave us a key and some vague directions to the subbasement.

It wasn't dusty or damp or covered in cobwebs as I'd imagined. There was a cement stairwell leading down to a fire door, beyond which was a dimly lit but clean corridor with several doors. One led to a boiler room, and one led to a room that housed the circuit breakers for the library. Both of those had red signs indicating they were off-limits to unauthorized personnel. The third door had a black-and-white sign that said Historical Archives.

Inside was just a small room with shelves of filing against three of the four walls. Beneath the shelves was a table that acted as a little desk. There were three orange plastic chairs, and several long fluorescent lights flickered overhead. The librarian had given us a reference list of the archive materials that gave the description of each file and its corresponding number.

"What exactly are we looking for?" Jac asked. I took the reference list from her and plopped down in one of the orange chairs.

"I don't know," I said, scanning the list. It was three pages long, and the print was small enough that I had to squint. "I'm hoping I'll know it when I see it."

"Are there any files having to do with the music program?"

"I don't see any. There's nothing about scholarships, nothing about music."

"Let me look," Jac said.

I handed the list to her impatiently. How was I supposed to help Suzanne, how was I supposed to get her out of my life, if I didn't know what she needed?

"Here's a file about the construction of the McClaren Music Wing," Jac said.

"We don't need to know about construction," I said. "How is that going to help us?"

"Well, it's the only file on this whole list that has the word *music* in it. We might as well go through it."

Jac examined the shelves, then picked a brown file box and pulled it out. She set it on the table and pulled out a stack of papers. I took some off the top and began to sift through them.

"It's all about this building ceremony, the opening of the new music wing, blah-blah-blah. Press releases. Newspaper clippings."

"They constructed a new gym, auditorium, and music wing in 1970," Jac read, from something similar she had found. "Not so new anymore."

"None of this . . ." I stopped. Something in one of the newspaper clippings had caught my eye.

"Wait, listen to this," I said. "Where the original school music room was located, two exterior walls were knocked down and the space expanded to accommodate the current library."

"Their current, or our current?" Jac asked.

"Both, I guess," I said. "Jac, don't you see? The point is, what is part of the library today used to be the old music room. That could be the connection to Suzanne that we're looking for. It makes sense she would have a bond to the old music room here. What it doesn't explain is why that connection remained after she died. What is stopping her from moving on?"

"I once saw a special on the History Channel about this hotel that burned in the 1940s, and when they rebuilt it the new floors were twelve inches higher than the original floors. And occasionally people would see ghosts walking down the corridors, and the ghosts were always cut off at the knees."

I sifted through the rest of the papers as Jac spoke, but nothing else caught my eye.

"Do you get it, Kat? The ghosts were walking on the *original* floors, which is why they looked cut off at the knees. Because the new floors —"

"Jac, check that box and see if there's anything else in it," I said.

"But do you get it, Kat? The ghosts were still walking in the old footprint of the building."

I reached over and grabbed the file box.

"I get it, Jac." Then I turned the box upside down over my head and shook it. A legal-size envelope fluttered past my gaze and landed neatly in Jac's lap.

"Hey," Jac said, but she didn't pick it up, so I reached over and grabbed it. The envelope was thin, and when I opened it there was only one page inside. I drew it out gently as the paper was old and yellowed.

When I read what was typed at the top of the paper, I gave a low whistle.

"The Suzanne Wittencourt Bennis Memorial Music Scholarship," I read.

"Wittencourt?" asked Jac.

"This looks like guidelines and requirements for the scholarship fund. An appointed judge to be chosen by the school board . . . annual scheduled audition . . . then there's a listing here for the names of the recipients. But there's only one winner's name listed, for 1961. A Dennis Rathberger. Where's 1962? Where are the other winners of the scholarship?"

"Maybe they opened a new file each year," Jac said.

"Well, there's no listing of a file like that in the reference list. It's like it just stopped in 1961."

"Kat, they must have been related," Jac said.

"Who?"

Jac pointed to the heading I'd read out loud.

"Suzanne *Wittencourt* Bennis. How often do you hear the name Wittencourt? It can't be a coincidence. It doesn't seem like they could have been sisters — the ages aren't right. Maybe she was Suzanne's aunt? Or grandmother? Somehow, the scholarship, Suzanne, and Miss Wittencourt are linked together. And why didn't Miss Wittencourt tell me that they were related when we were talking about Suzanne? If Miss Wittencourt isn't telling us the whole story, how do we get more answers?"

I gathered up the papers and put them back in the file.

"We take it to Suzanne, Jac."

"We take it to Suzanne?"

I took a deep breath.

"We have the séance."

Chapter 13

I woke long before my alarm went off at four
the next morning. My mother wasn't thrilled
with letting me out the door while it was still
dark, but we compromised by agreeing she
would drive me to the few short blocks to
school. Jac was waiting by the outside doors
that led to the music practice rooms, which
were down the hallway in the opposite
direction of the library. My mother waited
until we had the door unlocked and had
dragged Jac's cello inside. She'd brought it
to give her presence there some validity,

since she'd told her mother she was practicing. I hesitated long enough to see my mother's car pull away before following Jac inside to the dim hallway.

There's something creepy about a school after dark, or in this case, just after dawn. Everything is the same, exactly as you left it at last bell the previous afternoon. Nothing has been moved, or repainted, or changed. The only sound anywhere is the noise of your own breath and your shoes squeaking. Somehow, you've caught the school in the middle of its other life, its dark life that goes on when all the students and teachers are home sleeping.

I saw this movie once about one of those jack-in-the-box toys, the kind where you crank the handle and a clown pops out. Even though the box played a merry little tune, and even though the clown had brightly colored clothes and a big red smile painted on his face, every time you saw the thing you knew, you just knew for a fact, that it was the very embodiment of evil. Sorry to say, that's how I felt about my school as I stood in the library in the dark hours of the morning. Jac, on the other hand, seemed unperturbed. The girl who routinely checked her food for biohazards, the girl who couldn't catch sight of a wasp across the street without flinching, the girl who wouldn't take the shortcut through the grass to gym because she thought a snake might bite her ankle, this very same girl seemed unconcerned that we might well have blundered into the gates of hell, where the spawn of evil was even now waiting to ambush us from behind the display of books on knot making.

"So, what do we do here?" Jac asked. Her small dark outline made her look like a doll in the dim light. "Shall we go sit at the table where we first saw her? Is there a setup? Do you have some kind of crystal ball? I guess we have to chant, right? Oh, man, I ate before I left my house! Were we supposed to fast for twenty-four hours?"

I stared at my friend.

"What have you been reading?" I demanded. "*Dialoguing with the Dead for Dummies?* Where are you getting this stuff?"

Jac looked sheepish. "I didn't read anything. There might have been . . . I might have seen a little bit of a movie last night."

"A little bit of a movie? What movie?"

"It was called *Tombstone Shadows After Dark.* It was actually pretty good. It was about this girl who's being haunted by the shape of a tombstone that hangs over her head whenever she —"

Jac, please!" I said, irritated. "This isn't the Sci-Fi Channel, this is my life."

"I know that," Jac said, defensively. "But the girl in the movie, who was the same girl who was in that thing with Hilary Duff, the one where they go to Italy and she meets the guy on the motorcycle Vespa thing and he turns out to be some kind of Italian rock god —"

"Jac!"

"No, not her, but the *other* girl, the dark-haired one!"

"Shhhhh!" I hissed.

Jac stopped talking.

I was getting that feeling again. The indescribable feeling that probably has thirty words for it in some other language but not one single word in English to indicate my scalp beginning to prickle, my heart pounding, the blood rushing to my face, and my hands involuntarily reaching out in front of me, to feel for something or keep something away, I'm not sure which. The air grew charged, the way it feels when you walk by a waterfall. The silence grew louder, like it might suck the dark clear out of the room.

I felt a sharp pain in my right arm, emanating from my elbow. A quick glance indicated the cause of the pain was four of Jac's fingers, which she was digging into my arm as if her life depended on it.

"Ow," I whispered.

"Do you hear that?" she whispered back.

I heard it as soon as she said something. A faint, high-pitched melody, pure and childlike.

"It's Bach."

"What's back?"

Jac shook her head.

"That music. It's by Bach. I know that piece. I've played it on the cello."

Even my musically unschooled ear could identify the instrument playing the Bach piece as a flute.

"It's Suzanne," I said quietly. But how was Jac able to hear it?

The sound abruptly stopped as soon as I spoke.

"What does she want us to do?" Jac asked.

"Come on, let's go to the back table. That's where I've seen her both times."

We walked gingerly through the library. A pink light was beginning to glow outside, but inside it was still pretty dark.

Somewhere over by the magazine rack something rustled. A little more light was coming through the window now, and I could see a dark, featureless shape several feet away.

"Suzanne?" I whispered. But what I was looking at, the blobby black shape that seemed to be floating several feet in the air, did not have Suzanne's familiar bony outline. A feeling of dread crept into my throat, but I was absolutely paralyzed. I don't think I could have moved a muscle if my life depended on it. And I didn't want to tell Jac that something felt wrong. Selfishly, I was afraid she might run away and leave me. I felt it was important that we leave immediately, that we run from the building before the dark shapeless form came any closer. Saw us. Knew who we were.

A rustle again, like feet shuffling through leaves. Jac made a little weepy noise in her throat. Yeah, watching *Tombstone Shadows After Dark* must not seem like it had been such a good idea now. The dark shape still didn't move — it just hung there like a punching bag suspended from the ceiling. Around it, things seemed distorted, like it was sucking the light right out of space.

"Suzanne?" I whispered. And I'm not ashamed to say it — I was now seriously and dangerously freaked out.

"Kat, something doesn't feel right," Jac whispered. Give the girl a prize — she'd hit the nail on the head. I was ready to grab Jac's hand and race right on out of there when I heard something else, something I recognized. Suzanne Bennis's voice, coming from somewhere behind me.

"Why?" it half whispered, half breathed.

Jac's fingernails sank into my arm again. It felt like they were digging right down to the bone. I was actually glad for the pain — it gave me something to focus on.

"Suzanne, we're here to help you," I called. "Tell us what you need."

"Why?" came the voice again.

"To help you leave. Something is keeping you here. Help us help you to go," I said.

"Why did you stop?" said the voice.

"I haven't stopped, Suzanne. I'm right here. Can you tell me what it is that's preventing you from leaving?"

There was a long silence. I cleared my throat, and Jac flinched.

"Suzanne?"

"There is pain. There is guilt. Why did she stop?"

"Suzanne, I don't understand," I said, frustrated. "Whose pain? Why did who stop what?"

And why couldn't I see her? I had to stand my ground and find out how to help Suzanne. But the feeling of dread in my throat had become terror, because Suzanne's voice was not coming from the saclike shape hovering darkly. Whatever that thing was, it was something entirely different. My heart hammered in my chest. Suzanne's spirit was speaking to me, but there was something else with Jac and me in the library, too. Something bad.

"She is blameless," whispered Suzanne. Her voice sounded drained, as if she was drawing on all her energy to project it to me. "If she could hear me, she might understand. Bring her, if you think you can. But why, why has she stopped?"

"She's not making any sense," I whispered to Jac. "She keeps talking about someone's pain, then asking why she's stopped."

"I don't get it, either," Jac replied, her voice close to my ear.

"Tell her to stop is to die," the voice came

again. Suzanne sounded like she was slipping away.

"Suzanne, please explain! I don't understand what you're asking me!" I cried.

I heard an electric sound, a buzzing like a connection gone bad.

"Bring her, if you can. She will hear. But she must understand what it means to stop forever."

Suzanne Bennis's voice just switched off then, like somebody had hit the POWER switch on a television. Across the room, some of the overhead lights flickered on, then off again. I could feel it in my gut — Suzanne had left again, and our communication with her was over.

And yet the dark, formless shape still hung there in front of our table. I heard a buzzing again, this time like the sound of a thousand flies descending on something rotten. Something far beyond my power to deal with, something that wasn't seeking anything as innocent as communication.

"Kat . . ."

I didn't even bother trying to reply to Jac. I grabbed her by the arm and dragged her by the chair, sprinting in the direction of the door. Jac didn't need any encouragement — she quickly regained her balance and was through the door ahead of me. We ran like a couple of spooked rabbits, all the way down the hallway and out the door toward the parking lot, now pink and golden in the postsunrise light.

We kept running, just to be on the safe side. We didn't stop until we'd crossed the entire parking lot and jumped the fence of the preschool playground next door. I skidded to a halt by the giant wooden pirate ship, its ladders and slides still wet with dew. Jac had crouched in a nearby sandbox, where she found a green plastic shovel and was brandishing it in front of her.

Jac was practically hyperventilating, tears spilling down around her pointy nose.

"It's okay, Jac. We're okay now. It's okay."

"I feel sick. I felt something bad back there. My cello is still in there! What . . . just . . . happened?" Jac spluttered between breaths.

I shook my head. I wasn't going to pretend I knew if I didn't. If this was what your average séance was going to be like, I wasn't sure I could handle it. But something told me that this was anything but an average séance. There was something else in the library trying to block Suzanne from communicating, something sucking the energy as fast as she could muster it. Had Jac felt it, too?

Jac peered at me from the sandbox, but she didn't move. Sitting there on her butt in the sand holding the little shovel, she looked about six years old. It would have been funny if it hadn't been for the whole threatening brush with the underworld thing. A yellow butterfly fluttered innocently past Jac's head. She jumped and shrieked, flailing at it with her little shovel. Fortunately, in her terror her aim was not good.

"Jac, breathe! Come on, we're okay now. We're okay. That was just a butterfly."

Jac gave a little shudder and looked around her, like there might be an entire legion of pale yellow butterflies just behind her, waiting for the right moment to gnaw her head off.

"You said you heard music," I said.

Jac nodded. "When we walked in. It was

a Bach piece. I know it really well. It was definitely Bach's 'Ave Maria' on the flute."

"But you didn't hear Suzanne speak?"

Jac shook her head.

"The music stopped when we went to the table. Something smelled bad. Sour. But I never heard anything else. What did Suzanne say?"

"She said there was pain and guilt keeping her here. And she said something about if we brought 'her,' she would be able to hear, and she would understand. I think she meant Miss Wittencourt. But then she kept asking why she had stopped. It didn't make any sense. She kept saying, 'Why has she stopped?' And at one point, she said something like to stop was like dying. So wait, you definitely heard her playing, but you couldn't hear her when she spoke?"

Jac nodded.

"And you didn't see the . . . You never saw her? When I did. Nothing, until you heard Suzanne play?" I pressed.

"I don't know what I heard," Jac said. "I heard Bach's 'Ave Maria' on the flute."

"You heard Suzanne Bennis playing," I corrected.

"But I'm not a medium! Why would I be able to hear her playing?"

"My mother says mediums are people whose hard-wiring is extremely sensitive to different light and energy frequencies. Maybe a musician is hardwired to be extremely sensitive to music. You heard Suzanne play because music is your gift."

Jac seemed to mull this over. I touched her on the arm.

"Jac, maybe it isn't just because of me that Suzanne reached out and tried to communicate. Maybe she felt your gift for music. Maybe she was responding to both of us. Me because I'm sensitive to spirits, and you because you're sensitive to music."

Jac nodded again.

"Jac, why do you think Suzanne kept telling me not to let her stop? I don't even know Miss Wittencourt. What could she have stopped doing that I would know about?"

Jac looked down at her hands for a long time.

"I don't think Suzanne was talking about Miss Wittencourt stopping, Kat," she said after a while.

"Then . . ." I faltered.

"I think Suzanne was talking about me."

Chapter 14

We had relocated to the cafeteria when the smell of the before-school breakfast program wafted over the sandbox. Jac and I sat together at our usual midlist spillover table, but for once Jac's cello wasn't with us. Jac was so freaked out by our early morning dialogue with the dead that she wouldn't go back to the library to get her instrument. Not until the librarian and a few signature members of the Computer Club were there, the lights on, and the sun higher in the sky. She didn't seem concerned that something would happen to it. She insisted that nobody in their right mind under the age of forty-one cared about an old cello.

"So you're saying Suzanne was talking about the fact that you stopped playing the cello?" I asked for the fifth time.

"It's not that I think it's all about me," Jac said, spearing a hunk of scrambled eggs that escaped from her fork before it could reach her mouth. "Just that part she was saying about 'Why did she stop.'"

"Why?"

"Something Miss Wittencourt said once, at the very beginning when I was first introduced to her. It might have even been my first lesson with her. Her first question, no beating around the bush, was, "Why did you stop?" I didn't answer her. And like I told you, I didn't play anything. I just sat there. I kept waiting for a lecture, or to be asked to leave, but she just accepted it, that I wasn't playing. She didn't nag or anything. And she only said one other thing to me that day. She said something like, 'We can do this for now, Miss Jacqueline, but don't write off your future. For some, to stop is to die.' Something like that. It was the same thing you heard Suzanne say. 'Why did you stop? To stop is to die.' That's why I think Suzanne was talking about me."

I peeled an orange and mulled over this information.

"Okay. Let's go with it. Suzanne in some way is aware that you've stopped playing, and that fact is meaningful to her. We also know that her relative, Miss Wittencourt, now specializes in teaching students who are having trouble playing. Like she's devoted her life to bringing musicians back to music."

"Right," Jac said.

"Well, what if the *reason* Miss Wittencourt has this specialty is that Suzanne herself stopped playing?"

"I guess it's possible."

"So the question then is, why *did* Suzanne stop playing?"

"Sorry, no disrespect intended, honor to the dead and all, but duh, Kat. Because she *died*."

"Are you making a joke?" I said. I squeezed my orange too hard, and it squirted me in the eye.

"I'm totally serious. That picture we saw in the yearbook, it was probably taken not too long before Suzanne got sick, and she's standing there *playing*. Not looking blocked or stricken by stage fright or anything. I think the problem is that Suzanne got sick, really sick. Too sick to be saved."

I blotted at my eye with a napkin.

"What's the name of the thing we think Suzanne died of again?"

"Meningitis," said Jac, taking another stab at her eggs.

"And that's, like, a really contagious thing?"

"Yep."

"I'm still not getting the whole picture. Suzanne said something about if we could bring her here, she would understand or something."

"Fat chance," said Jac, dropping a forkful of eggs again. She made an exasperated sound and switched to a spoon.

"Fat chance?"

"Getting Miss Wittencourt here. She barely ever goes anywhere. She says it's because she doesn't drive, but I get the idea she really doesn't like going out. One of her students does her grocery shopping for her."

"Well, why?"

"You know, it hasn't really come up in conversation, Kat. Like, 'Oh, by the way, Miss Wittencourt, while we're sitting here in silence listening to me *not* play, what's up with you not liking to leave the house?'"

"You could find a nicer, more casual way to ask," I said. "Seems like she might welcome a fresh topic of conversation."

Students were starting to trickle into the cafeteria — ones who came early because their parents had to drop them off before eight on their way to work, or other complicated reasons I wasn't interested in knowing. One or two of them seemed to find Jac and me amusing in some way. I ignored the snickers as an unpleasant by-product of junior high existence.

"Wait a minute," Jac said suddenly. "I have an idea."

"Spill it," I said, eagerly.

"I think it's about the music fund, Kat."

"The music fund?"

"A music fund is like a memorial. One like this is, anyway. Okay. Suzanne dies, right? And here she was this gifted musician, and now her life has been cut short before she could really come into her own. So her grandmother or her aunt or whatever Miss Wittencourt is to her besides her teacher, establishes this music fund, which is named in her memory. So the idea is, every year some new young musician will get some help, and at the same time Suzanne's memory will be honored and her name will stay in people's minds."

"Makes sense," I said. A few Satellite Girls had come into the cafeteria and were looking right at me. They were *definitely* laughing. I checked my reflection in Jac's shiny silver thermos but didn't see any obvious material for mockery.

"But the fund didn't survive. No student is being chosen to win it every year. Or if they were, they aren't now. I mean, that's kind of like the equivalent of someone going into the graveyard and knocking down your headstone."

Jac obviously had headstones on the brain, but what she said made more sense than any theory I'd been able to come up with.

"Well, I know two things we can probably find answers to. I'm going to find out more about the history of that music fund, and when they stopped awarding it to students."

"I could find that out," Jac said, looking a

little indignant. "I am a musician, after all. Well, a *lapsed* musician."

"Which should make you much less inclined to be poking around asking about it," I said. "What if they suddenly ask you to audition?"

"Oh," Jac said, her face falling.

"Anyway, you have to find out from Miss Wittencourt what exactly happened with Suzanne."

"I don't know — that's kind of a tall order. I guess I can try," Jac said.

Two more Satellite Girls walked in. Stared at me. Giggled. Then two football players came in behind them. Also noticed us. Also seemed amused.

"Okay," I said suddenly. "Something is going on."

"I think we've established that," Jac

said, rolling her eyes as she unsuccessfully chased a bite of scrambled eggs around her plate with a spoon.

"No, like, right now," I said. My heart was starting to pound, and I was starting to experience some serious paranoia. "Am I fully dressed? Do I appear normal to you?"

Because the whole thing had the air of a dream when you find yourself at school in your pajamas. Or worse, without them.

"Of course," Jac said. "Darn these stupid eggs, anyway. They keep falling apart every time I try to take a bite."

"I need to get out of here. We need to get out of here," I said firmly.

Jac looked up at me, her face registering surprise and confusion. But when I got up, she got up with me.

"It's probably safe to go back to the library now, anyway," she said. "Gotta get the ball and chain before someone drags it to lost and found."

An unlikely scenario. But I was just glad to get away from the looks and the snickers. I felt better as soon as we were in the hallway, but my stomach still sensed something bad going on. I went down the hallway at something just short of a jog. Jac was getting breathless trying to keep up with me.

We passed the bio lab and turned down the hall where the seventh-grade lockers were. Almost instantly, I came to a dead stop.

"What are you doing?" Jac asked.

I didn't answer — just tried to assess things from a distance.

"Kat, what are you. . . . Hey, is that your locker?"

One locker, looking solitary and forlorn in a long line of otherwise unadorned lockers, had been decorated. It was, as Jac had so intelligently surmised, *my* locker. A bemused-looking Quinn Irvin was examining the outside of it.

I walked slowly toward it as Quinn turned and began walking toward me. Her face broke into a good-natured grin when she caught sight of me.

"Greetings, o great Katslavina," Quinn said mysteriously, bowing to me slightly as she walked past.

"What?" Jac murmured.

But we had both reached my locker now and could see for ourselves.

The locker had been draped in one of those beaded curtains, like the kind of sixties hippie, groovy sort of beaded curtains. Similar, I have to say, to several hanging in my very own home. The beads framed a hand-drawn poster of a crystal ball, behind which stood a turban-wearing girl who bore no small resemblance to me. Giant lettering around the image read:

SEEK AUDIENCE WITH THE ALL-SEEING KATSLAVINA.
ALL WILL BE REVEALED IN HER CRYSTAL BALL AND HER TAROE CARDS OF WISDOM. NOW APPEARING AT THE COUNTY FAIR, IN THE BOOTH NEXT TO THE DOG-FACED LADY.

ONLY $1 PER READING!

"You have got to be kidding me," I spluttered. "She didn't even spell tarot cards right. Geez."

Jac was staring at the poster with her mouth hanging open.

"Who did this? Do you think it was Shoshanna?" Jac asked. "Because of the Dance Decoration Committee thing?"

"It could have been," I said. "Seems more Brooklyn Bigelow's style, actually."

I reached up and ripped the poster down. The beaded curtain came with it, one of the strings snapping. Purple and blue plastic beads rolled in eight directions.

"Oh, great," I exclaimed. My voice broke, and I felt the terrifying, unstoppable sensation of a huge sob forming in my throat.

"Give me that," Jac said quickly. She pulled the armful of bead strings and poster from my hands and ran to the closest garbage can, where she stuffed the whole mess in with impressive speed. As she made her way back to me she collected the stray beads from the floor as if she were an Olympic-caliber blueberry picker.

"I'm such a freak," I moaned as Jac put the beads in her pocket.

"Kat, don't," Jac said.

"Seriously! I'm a loser, and now I'm a joke!"

Jac stomped her tiny foot on the ground, something I'd never seen her do before. Something, actually, I'd never seen *anyone* do before.

"Don't you dare even try that, with me of all people!"

I looked at Jac in surprise. Her outburst had the fortunate effect of stopping my tears, which as far as I knew could be controlled by no known force of humanity once they started rolling down my face.

"She came to you, Kat. After all these years, she came to *you*. Was it because you're an ordinary, fit-in-with-the-crowd, make-no-waves Satellite Girl? *No.* It was because you're special. Because you have a *gift.* Both of us have gifts, Kat, that most people don't have. And okay, yeah, fine. That sets us apart from the drones and the trendies. That calls attention to us from the haters. That's the price we pay, and don't tell me for a minute you'd rather be like them than who you are. Who your mother is. Don't tell me for *one second* that you'd trade it all in to be just like everybody else."

And right out of nowhere, I really felt it. That it was real. I was a medium. I had the spirit sight just like my mother, and it was going to be my life, which would be different from anyone else's. And that might actually be the way I wanted it.

That knowledge, and Jac's solid presence, made the long day of people calling me Katslavina and asking where my crystal ball was endurable. And even though I felt embarrassed and defensive and humiliated, I just laughed when people teased me and acted like they were paying me some big compliment. Brooklyn Bigelow made the most noise about it, but only when she was in a crowd of Satellite Girls. And though she talked frequently and loudly about how hard this was going to make Shoshanna laugh, I never actually saw her crack a smile. In fact, she seemed to be ignoring Brooklyn. I wondered if they were on the outs.

Later, after gym, I saw Brooklyn standing by herself at the sink. When she saw my reflection in the mirror standing silently behind her, she backed away from me like I was a knife-wielding psycho. In the fluorescent light her highlights looked greenish and fake. I could tell she was nervous I might start chanting another one of my spells. As awful a person as Brooklyn was, I still felt bad about disrespecting my gift in that way, so I let her scurry away without saying anything.

Much later that night, when I was lying in bed trying to sort out all the clues Suzanne Bennis had given me, I remembered that after she'd disappeared, after her voice had stopped, that there had been *something else* still in the library. Something that filled me with such deep fear that I haven't even told my best friend about it.

When the sun came up, I still hadn't slept.

Chapter 15

By the time Jac and I had both obtained answers to our respective questions, Friday's dance was almost upon us. I hadn't encountered any resistance in pressing for information about the Bennis Music Fund. It was more that the people I asked, starting with the librarian, had only the vaguest idea that such a fund had ever existed. Tracking down additional documentation turned out to be something like a treasure hunt.

Finally, a librarian's aide found the papers misfiled in a box of paperwork suggesting athletic scholarship programs. These papers told another chapter in the story. As we thought from what we'd seen in the archives, Miss Wittencourt had only held auditions in the first year after Suzanne's death. After that, the activity stopped altogether. Apparently no one ever thought to look into it. Probably things were the same back then — most people cared about the sports program way more than the music program. But an enterprising secretary in the principal's office who was known to watch far too much *Law and Order* decided to play detective and discovered that the account with the Bennis Music Fund money was still active at the bank. And apparently, since it had never been tapped into, the balance had grown to be quite a healthy amount.

Jac made another special, non-cello visit to Miss Wittencourt to broach the topic of

Suzanne. She brought a copy of the old yearbook with her, along with a photocopy we'd made of the original scholarship document from the historical archives. It was a risky move, but Jac felt seeing the things might inspire Miss Wittencourt to open up even more. The gamble paid off, and Jac called me after dinner to report.

"Did you find out anything new?" I asked eagerly.

"Oh, Kit Kat. When I'm done talking, you'll wonder if there's anything I *didn't* find out."

This sounded promising.

"Spit it out," I urged impatiently.

But Jac wanted to take a moment to savor her secrets.

"I realized after I handed in my bio project that I hadn't listed the cities on the bibliography. Did you list cities?"

"JAC!"

The phone accurately transmitted the sound of Jac's small, tolerant sigh.

"Okay," she said. "Gosh, where do I begin?"

"Pick a place, and go with it," I said, gritting my teeth.

"Geez. Okay. So I just went and knocked on her door tonight, and she seemed happy to see me, and we went into the living room where we always go. And I put the yearbook and the scholarship file on the table and told her I'd found them in the library. She picked up the yearbook and opened it straight to Suzanne's memorial page. She looked at it for a long time. And then she picked up the scholarship document. As soon as she saw it, her eyes filled with tears. I felt really bad then. But that opened something in her, and she looked at me and shook her head and said it was her fault, and she should never have let the scholarship lapse after that."

"After what?"

"I wondered the same thing. And I wasn't sure what the right question was. So I asked Miss Wittencourt if Suzanne Bennis had died of meningitis, and I pointed out that her middle name was Wittencourt. And she looked up at me kind of surprised, I guess surprised I knew or something. And she nodded, and said yes, it had happened about a year after she started teaching Suzanne. And that Suzanne was her favorite student, and that she also was her niece."

"So Miss Wittencourt *was* her aunt!"

"Yep. She talked about her sister, Suzanne's mom. I guess the mom and Miss Wittencourt didn't really get along. Miss Wittencourt knew Suzanne had this great musical gift, and she kept nagging her sister to let her give Suzanne lessons. She had these dreams, she said, that Suzanne would play these big concerts. The kinds of concerts Miss Wittencourt played, way back. And she started pushing Suzanne really hard, because she wanted her to succeed at the highest level, where only the very best musicians in the world go. Suzanne's mom didn't like it, and she and Miss Wittencourt had some kind of falling out. Then Miss Wittencourt told me that Suzanne had died because of *her*."

"Miss Wittencourt said it was her own fault Suzanne died? What about the meningitis?"

"I know. She said there was this important audition Suzanne and another student were supposed to go to. For a famous music school, I think, or something. They were supposed to play a duet. Remember when I could hear that melody by Bach in the library? The one Suzanne was playing? I've played it too. 'Ave Maria.' Anyway, the girl Suzanne was to play the duet with had called to say she wasn't feeling well. Suzanne thought they ought to skip the audition, but Miss Wittencourt said she got really mad at both of them and insisted they go, because a chance like this didn't come around very often."

"And?"

"And according to Miss Wittencourt, the other girl came down with full-blown meningitis the day after the audition. Suzanne got it a few days later. The first girl eventually got better. But as we know, Suzanne didn't."

"So Miss Wittencourt blamed herself for Suzanne getting sick and dying."

"Exactly," Jac said. "Because she said she knew there was an outbreak of it. Everyone knew. She didn't know the other girl had it, but she knew a lot of young people did. A lot of people wouldn't go anywhere in public for fear of catching it. But Miss Wittencourt made Suzanne go to the audition. She said that later her sister, Suzanne's mother, said, 'You killed my daughter.' And she and her sister never spoke again.

"It was so strange, Kat. I couldn't believe Miss Wittencourt was just up and telling me all of it. Like she'd been waiting all these years for someone to find out and ask. She said she just never got over the fact that she wouldn't hear Suzanne play again. She kept hearing that horrible thing her sister said. And every time she helped a student who was thinking about stopping playing, she thought it would get better, but it never did. She said that a few times. That she just couldn't get past the idea of never hearing Suzanne play again."

"But we heard her. She is still playing."

"I know, right? But what was I gonna tell her? That Suzanne's spirit is still bound to the place the music room used to be?"

"Yes, okay, point taken, genius. But we have to find some way to get her to the school, Jac, so she can hear Suzanne play."

"Look, I think I've done enough for the night. Miss Wittencourt has confessed her life story to me, I've confessed it to you, and I've got to get through forty pages of European history reading before *American Idol* comes on."

It amazed me, really, that Jac watched *American Idol.* Her appetite for pop culture was absolutely insatiable. The fact that she was a lapsed cello genius made what might otherwise be of grave concern into an adorable eccentricity.

"All right, Maestra," I said. "I know your day doesn't straighten out until you see Simon Cowell bullying some lifestyle-challenged sixteen-year-old."

"Thank you, Voodoo Mama. Anyway, we'll have hours to talk about this at the dance tomorrow night."

My jaw dropped.

"What?"

"The dance, Kat. The one decorated with gems, stars, and moons that, thanks to me, you had no part in cutting out."

"What in the world makes you think I'd go to that dance, Jac? You yourself said you knew I had no intention of going."

"Yeah, but that was before," Jac replied.

"Before *what?*"

"Two things. First and foremost, before one of the Satellite Girls attempted to humiliate you into a permanent state of embarrassment. The only way to prove you weren't scarred for life by that little prank is to show up, acting happy as a clam, at the dance."

"You can't be serious," I said.

"Oh, but I am," Jac said. "And now there's a second reason. This pre-concert talent show thing that our good friend Shoshanna is heading up. Anyone, including you, taking a music or drama class or auditing an arts program, which I happen to be doing, gets extra credit for attending this optional event."

"What are you, like, reading from a *flyer?*"

"I am, in fact, reading from a flyer. I need this extra credit. For obvious reasons. I'm not doing any of the other extra credit things — the concert, the master class, the cross-instrument youth group. It's going to be hard enough to explain to my mother why I haven't gotten twenty extra credits. I need to go sit at this thing and get this credit. And you, you need to face your fears, Voo-doo Mama."

"I don't know, Jac, I really don't. When is this pre-dance talent show thing?"

"It's at seven, in the library."

"The library."

"Yep. Then the dance picks up in the gym at eight."

I truly did not want to go to the dance. I wasn't sure I agreed with Jac's assessment that I needed to make a brave showing. As far as I was concerned, I'd already *done* that. But an idea was forming in my head.

"I guess I could at least stop by the library show thing with you," I said.

"I knew you'd see it my way. Gotta hop. Catch you tomorrow in school."

I said good night and hung up. I had already done my history reading, and I wasn't interested in *American Idol*, so I was free to open my mind to the idea that had begun to form and to wait for it to blossom.

So I ended up sacrificing a coveted Friday night, and a nice rainy one at that, to go sit in the library and experience the so-called talents of several of my schoolmates. Jac hadn't seemed to notice that I'd already been at the library for a while when she arrived. And if I seemed to be checking the clock frequently or casting many glances back toward the door, Jac didn't find this behavior unusual in any way.

"Did you sign in?" she asked. "You have to sign in to get the extra credit."

"I don't *need* the extra credit," I said. "I'm making this sacrifice purely for you, my friend."

"Don't talk to me about sacrifice," Jac countered. "I'm missing a two-hour special on E Television called *Celebrity Shoplifters.* Who knows *when* they'll broadcast that again."

"Who is performing at this thing, anyway?" I asked.

"As of this morning, nobody was," Jac said. "Which apparently got Shoshanna into major recruiting gear. Now there are two acts scheduled. Lance Silverstein is going to perform a scene from *SuperSize Me.* I could not care less. The credit goes on my academic record, and my mother gets off my back a little."

"*SuperSize Me?* But that's a documentary. How do you perform a scene from a documentary?"

Jac shrugged. "Not my problem. And then, some of Shoshanna's friends are going to sing 'You Are the Wind Beneath My Wings.'"

"Please tell me you're not serious."

"They wanted to sing 'Lady Marmalade,' but they got censored."

"This is ridiculously lame."

"Judge not lest ye be judged, Voodoo Mama. Think of it as *American Idol* with credit."

Actually, that's not how I thought of it at all. I cast another discreet look back toward the door.

Shoshanna Longbarrow had gotten up

on the makeshift stage by the windows, where her simple presence caused a hush to fall about the room. Though she hadn't quite returned to the full-on celestial entity she'd been before her grandmother's funeral, Shoshanna certainly had a command of the room. Most of the audience members were Drama Club nerds, Satellite Girls, and a small smattering of jocks and midlist spill-overs. I was surprised, actually, how many people Shoshanna had roped into coming. There must have been about sixty people in the library altogether.

Shoshanna was already mid-speech.

". . . of course, make sure you sign the clipboard by the librarian's desk if you'd like to receive official academic credit for attending this event from the art and music department. Okay, that said, I'd like to go ahead and welcome our first performer,

Lance Silverstein, whom many of you know from his roof-raising performance as a singing and dancing President Franklin Delano Roosevelt in our fall production of *Annie*. Lance is going to be performing a scene from the documentary film blockbuster *SuperSize Me*. And while Lance is getting ready, I'd like to remind you all that new acts are welcome at any time, no pre-announcement necessary. It would be fab to have more than just two performances up here tonight, guys."

Shoshanna looked very stern and scanned the audience for potential last-minute performers, causing an entire row of Satellite Girls to begin squirming and checking the floor for nonexistent dropped earrings.

As it turned out, Lance was performing a reenactment of the scene where Morgan Spurlock, having consumed a double bacon cheeseburger, SuperSized Coke, and SuperSized fries, is languishing in his car as his stomach begins to make sounds usually indicating impending digestive doom. Lance bravely and weakly raised a hand to signal to the camera crew that he had recovered sufficiently from his post-feeding stupor to consume the remaining three bites of his burger. Moments later, he was miming rolling down a car window and vomiting explosively onto the imaginary sidewalk. The audience erupted in wild applause. Lance stood up and took a number of bows and might have continued to do so if several Satellite Girls, led by Brooklyn, hadn't literally pushed him off the stage.

"We will be singing 'You Are The Wind Beneath My Wings,'" Brooklyn uttered breathlessly into the microphone.

I gave another look in the direction of the door, and this time I saw what I was looking for.

"Gotta pee, be right back," I whispered to Jac, and hurriedly left my seat before she could respond.

I picked my way through the audience and slipped out through the door. My eyes hadn't been playing tricks on me — she *was* here. In the hallway stood Miss Wittencourt, propping up a large object beside her. It wasn't Jac's ball and chain — there simply hadn't been any way to get *that*, but it was a cello. When I called Miss Wittencourt earlier in the evening, I hadn't exactly given her the full story. But I'd mentioned our interest in Suzanne, my friendship with Jac, and a talent show scheduled to be performed in school that evening. I begged Miss Wittencourt to come and bring a cello with her, just in case Jac could be persuaded to play. To my astonishment, she'd agreed right away. I arranged for a taxi, and now here Miss Wittencourt stood, big as life, right in the hallway. I walked over to her and took her elegant, wrinkled hand in mine.

"Miss Wittencourt, I'm Kat. I'm Jac's friend. We spoke on the phone. Remember? Kat."

Miss Wittencourt nodded. "Yes, of course. I'm pleased to meet you. Is Miss Jacqueline inside?"

I nodded.

"Okay. I think if we do this right, we can convince Jac to get up there and play the cello tonight. If she does that, she's past her block, right?"

"If she can perform here, for these people, then, yes. She will have made a significant psychological step toward resuming her music," Miss Wittencourt replied.

"And that would be huge. I mean, wouldn't it? Did you say when someone has a gift like that, to stop is to die?"

Miss Wittencourt looked at me gravely. She pressed her lips together, and glanced into the library.

"Yes," she said, finally. "Yes, I did say that."

She was so much smaller than I'd thought. Almost Jac's size, with snow-white hair pinned up in a messy bun, and bright cornflower blue eyes.

"Because there's something else, Miss Wittencourt. If I can do what I hope I can do, there's something that you need to hear, also. Other than Jac, I mean."

Miss Wittencourt didn't really seem to

be listening to me. She was looking around through the library door as if she hadn't seen the room in decades. Which of course, she hadn't. The alarming shrill sounds of Satellite singing didn't seem to faze her. Miss Wittencourt took a tentative step inside.

My heart was beating so fast I thought it might fly right out of my chest. I hadn't anticipated being this nervous. But everything was moving forward now. Miss Wittencourt had reached the library door and stood, looking inside.

Showtime.

Chapter 16

I could see Jac in her seat, looking around for me, wondering why I hadn't come back from the bathroom. I ducked back into the shadows. I didn't want her to catch sight of me yet. The final, hideous verse of "Wind Beneath My Wings" had begun. I darted over to the stack where I'd first seen Suzanne. I stood between the stack and the wall, hidden from most of the audience.

"Suzanne," I whispered. "Suzanne Bennis. I need you. I've brought her."

She was there in a split second, her white blond braids swinging as if I'd caught her midjump.

Several thoughts zipped into my mind. That I could be wrong about it all. That my plan might not work. But Suzanne was staring intently at me with those bottomless, vacant eyes.

"I've brought Miss Wittencourt here, Suzanne. Where she can hear you. And when she hears you, you know that she'll be able to let you go."

"She is here?"

"I've brought her very close. You've got to play for her."

"The other one. Why did she stop?"

"That's another thing we're going to put right tonight. I don't think any people out there can hear you, because I believe you have to be highly musically gifted to pick up the sound. But Miss Wittencourt will be able to, I feel fairly certain. And I know that Jac can *hear* you when you play. She recognized that piece you were playing that morning in the library, 'Ave Maria.' I'm going to make her come up here and play with you. Just start playing. Somehow I'll convince her to join you. I don't think she would do it for herself, but if she thinks she's doing it because it will help you and Miss Wittencourt, there's a chance. Do you understand, Suzanne, what I'm saying?"

The strange, empty face nodded. Understand or not, there was no more time. The Satellite Girls had finished and were basking in a smattering of applause. I maneuvered around the stacks and over to Shoshanna's makeshift stage. Pushing my way in front of an indignant Brooklyn Bigelow, I took the microphone.

"There *is* one more performance tonight. A classical music piece. But before I introduce it, I want to tell you about a school program that's going to be restarted. It's a prize, actually, a music prize. It's called the Suzanne Wittencourt Bennis Music Fund. Suzanne Bennis was a flutist, a really, really, good one, who died in nineteen sixty when she was a senior. She never got to go on to study at a conservatory — never experienced the wonderful career she would have had."

I could see Jac's face, her mouth dropped in a perfect *O* of confusion, but I wouldn't let myself look at her for long. I had to do this exactly right. I looked off in the direction I'd left Suzanne and made a small gesture that she should come stand with me.

"Come now, Suzanne," I mumbled, my mouth turned away from the mic. "Bring your flute."

Then I put the microphone back in front of my mouth.

"The surprise I have to tell you about tonight is that to celebrate the reinstitution of the Suzanne Bennis Fund, a very special guest is here. Miss Wittencourt was a music teacher at this school before most of our parents even met. She was Suzanne Bennis's teacher, and she is the founder of the fund."

Miss Wittencourt was standing off to one side by the wall, squinting very hard into the lights and holding her cello beside her. I glanced over and saw that Suzanne was standing there, just onstage. She looked more flat than usual, more two-dimensional. As if the strain of summoning all this energy to communicate was draining her.

"Let's give her a round of applause, okay?"

The audience obediently clapped, accustomed by now to being ordered around. Miss Wittencourt gave a little wave.

"Okay, now without further ado. . . . You've seen her dragging her cello through the halls and in and out of the lunchroom. Now, to play Bach's 'Ave Maria,' and to audition for this year's Suzanne Wittencourt Bennis Music Fund, is Miss Jacqueline Gray."

Jac's mouth dropped open even more, and I could see her shaking her head violently in an unmistakable no. But Miss Wittencourt was pulling the cello up onstage as we'd planned, and I leaped off the platform and skidded on my knees over to Jac.

"You are out of your flipping mind; it is *not* going to happen!" she hissed.

"Jac, look," I said. "Onstage. Do you see her?"

Jac looked at where Suzanne stood, patiently holding her flute.

"No."

"Then you'll have to take my word for it — Suzanne is up there with her flute. I think she'll play. But she's not going to play without you," I said. "This is all about that last duet she played for her audition. That girl who gave her meningitis, she was a cellist, Jac. Miss Wittencourt told me. Now I've actually gotten Miss Wittencourt to school, and this is our *one* chance to set everything right. I just know Suzanne will play that duet with you, and Miss Wittencourt will hear. When she hears that Suzanne's music is still alive and with us, she'll let go of all that guilt. Jac, you've *got* to. For them. My gift brought Suzanne here, just like you said. But I can't do anything more. Only you can."

There was this really long pause then. I kept my mouth shut. I'd said exactly what needed to be said. No more, no less. It was up to Jac now. She was perfectly still for what seemed like forever.

Then, like she was moving in slow motion, like she was underwater, Jac got to her feet. I glanced up onstage and saw that Suzanne's empty eyes were following Jac's every move. Jac practically glided onstage. She took the cello, which Miss Wittencourt had removed from its case. Student and teacher exchanged a brief but intense look. Then Miss Wittencourt turned and stepped down, moving to stand off to the side against the wall.

"What's the holdup?" called a voice from behind me. "Is she going to play or not? We've got a *dance* to go to."

I whirled around to face the voice, which had come from Brooklyn.

"You be quiet," I hissed.

Brooklyn's face assumed its usual unpleasant shape. She sucked her cheeks in and pursed her lips as she narrowed her eyes.

"Or else what, Katslavina? Will you throw your crystal ball at me?"

"You'll have to just wait and see what I'll do," I said. "But I guarantee you won't like it."

Brooklyn stood up.

"This is over," she called over the heads of the audience. "Come on, people, let's go to the gym and get this party started!"

A few people started to get up, too. Satellite Girls, mostly. But Shoshanna motioned them to sit back down. Brooklyn, who had already made a great show of flouncing over to the door, made an explosive sound of anger.

"This show is history!" she called.

People started murmuring, looking around. Wondering if Brooklyn was right. Jac had taken a seat with her instrument and held her bow in hand, but she hadn't started playing. She looked frozen. Rigid.

"Come on, people!" Brooklyn called again.

People began to shuffle in their seats. A few stood up. Then I heard it. A high, clear strain of flute music. I recognized the line as the one we'd heard Suzanne play in the library. "Ave Maria."

Although to my knowledge not a single one of the students could see or hear Suzanne, something seemed nonetheless to still them. The entire audience fell silent as

Suzanne played the second bar, looking around to figure out why everyone had quieted down and what they were supposed to be seeing. Jac, looking hypnotized, lifted her bow. When Suzanne began playing the third bar, Jac joined in.

At the very first lines she played, the whole world seemed to drop away. Jac was playing a laddered structure of notes beneath Suzanne's "Ave Maria," a tune that itself sounded strangely familiar. I felt the vibration of the cello deep inside my chest, the place my mother called the heart chakra. The sound was so rich, so deep and pure, I honestly thought I might float out of my seat. I was completely and utterly mesmerized. As she played, Jac swayed slightly, her eyes closed. The music seemed to come effortlessly, the deep vibrations hanging overhead with an unsettling but beautiful intensity. It was the most beautiful sound I had ever heard in my life.

Her mother is right, I thought. *Jac is a genius.* Her gift was truly the very rarest of things. And the way she and Suzanne were playing together, it was as if they had become the same entity. Sometimes it was difficult to tell where the cello ended and the flute began.

It was a short piece, and it ended quietly and simply, with each instrument playing the same note. There was a long silence, then suddenly every person in that room was on their feet, clapping their hands and stamping their feet as if Bono himself had just walked onto the stage, with the rest of U2 in tow.

Jac didn't move an inch. She just sat there, her head bent down, holding her bow.

But Suzanne was looking past the audience. I turned to see Miss Wittencourt, her hands clasped together, a tear running down her face. The look on her face told me what I needed to know. Miss Wittencourt had heard. She had heard both her students play, one living, one not. Both quite simply brilliant.

The air was so charged with electricity I could feel my hair standing on end. The amount of energy that had gathered in the room was overwhelming. Something powerful, something unprecedented, had just happened. Even the Satellite Girls seemed to sense it. I looked back onstage, where Jac had still not moved. But Suzanne seemed to be transformed. As I stared at her, I literally saw life rush into her eyes. Her flat, unanimated features filled out. For one moment she really looked like a living, breathing person, as alive as she had ever been.

"Hey, who's that other girl?" I heard someone ask.

And that's when I heard a tremendous bang, and all the lights in the library, including some nobody knew about, instantly went out, leaving every last one of us in complete darkness.

If I'd thought of it, I might have actually included the lightning strike and the blackout in my plan. It was a very convenient way for Suzanne to disappear, for Jac to slowly come out of her coma, and for me to safely lead Miss Wittencourt out of the room. It really was a perfect touch.

But I hadn't thought of it. Most likely, in breaking out of her ghostly cycle, Suzanne had undergone some kind of energy transformation that messed with the electricity and acted like a lightning rod.

When the lights came back on a minute later, I had already groped my way to the door leading out to the corridor. Pulling her cello myself, I led Miss Wittencourt to the outside door at the end of the hall where I'd be able to see when her taxi arrived. She was still wiping tears from her face.

I felt strangely uncomfortable. This was the aspect of mediumship I knew the least about — how to interact with the living. Miss Wittencourt had just had a major emotional experience. After decades of blaming herself for bringing an end to her niece's music and life, she had heard that music and that sensed life again. She had understood that neither the student nor the music were gone in the permanent way she'd thought. But I didn't know what was expected of me now. I didn't know what Miss Wittencourt wanted me to say, or if she wanted to be left alone entirely with her thoughts. I was flying blind, and I felt helpless.

Outside I saw headlights, and the yellow dome light of the local taxi company. I opened the door and held it for Miss Wittencourt, motioning for the driver to come help load the cello into the trunk. As she began to walk by me, I touched her arm.

"Miss Wittencourt . . ." I faltered.

She stopped and looked at me with those bright blue eyes. She said nothing at all, but before she walked away she gave me a simple nod.

And I knew that nod meant yes. I heard. Yes. I understand. Yes. I see.

I had done my job, and I had done it well enough. I felt a little lump in my throat as I watched the driver help Miss Wittencourt into the taxi. I longed to see my mother, to tell her every single detail. I knew I'd done a good thing, and I wanted my mother's approval so badly I could hardly stop myself from running home that very moment. But there was more to do here.

Before I could walk back into the library to look for Jac, Shoshanna Longbarrow came out a door into the hallway, bumping right by me.

"Oh, Kat," she said. "Sorry. I didn't see you."

A week ago, I would have assumed Shoshanna was lying about being sorry, that she'd bumped into me deliberately just to show she could. But ever since Brooklyn had declared war on me, Shoshanna had seemed different. She'd been present several times when Brooklyn was indulging in some public trash-Kat sessions, but she'd never joined in. What had happened to change her?

"I'm sorry about your grandmother," I said suddenly. I hadn't planned to say anything, but after what I'd seen and helped accomplish that night, I felt like a different person.

"Yeah, thanks," Shoshanna said. Her eyes looked like they might be watering. "It's been . . . we were really close. But actually I'm feeling better these past few days, since I was able to . . . well, whatever."

I just stood there, having no idea what to else to say. Shoshanna made a move like she was about to go, then she hesitated.

"So, listen, that stuff Brooklyn's been saying about you and your mom," Shoshanna said. "I'm . . . not totally down with that. Brooklyn can be pretty vicious sometimes. I can't always control what she does.

But I'm going to tell her to lighten up, or whatever. She's getting really lame."

I was stunned. Shoshanna hadn't apologized for telling Brooklyn about the weirdness I call home. Shoshanna was queen of the Satellite Girls and she was going to remain that way. But the little she had just said to me really meant something. Shoshanna was no Jac Gray, and never would be. But she wasn't quite a Brooklyn Bigelow, either. And that was encouraging.

Shoshanna did start to walk away now.

"That was really fab, by the way, your getting Jac to play," she called over her shoulder. "At least we had *one* real talent in the show."

Then she swept away in the direction of the gym, no doubt to tackle the considerable work of Dance Decoration Maintenance.

This was turning out to be quite the night of the unexpected.

I finally found Jac in the gym, standing by the beverage table. I was eager to tell Jac all about Miss Wittencourt but was surprised to find that her face was red with anger.

"How *dare* you?" she hissed.

"What?"

"You know *exactly* what I mean. You were supposed to be my friend. You're the only one I told! How could you, of all people, pull that stunt on me?"

I was genuinely speechless.

"I . . . buh . . ."

"That was the lowest, dirtiest thing anyone has ever done to me, Kat. I thought I knew you. I thought we had an understanding."

"But Jac, you played. You *played!*"

"Well, you hardly gave me a choice, did you?"

"But . . . Jac, you got past your block. You *played*. You sounded like an angel! Isn't that a good thing?"

Jac's face was still bright red. I grabbed a plastic cup of Mountain Dew and handed it to her.

"You *tricked* me," she said, still sounding angry. But not quite so angry as before, if I was reading her right.

"I know, Jac. I know, and I'm sorry. I just got this idea, you know, after I heard the talent show was going to be in the library, where Suzanne was. I had no idea if I could pull it off. I just figured if I could get Miss Wittencourt to that library, Suzanne might play, but only if I could get *you* up there playing, too."

"Well, did it ever occur to you," Jac

spluttered, over-pronouncing every word, "to *ask* me about your little plan? Find out how I felt about taking a starring role? Instead of duping me like I'm on some episode of *Punk'd?* You know I have issues with playing!"

"But, Jac, you might have said no," I said, apologetically.

"Darn right I would have said no. Because I *didn't* want to do it!"

She downed the Mountain Dew in one gulp. Yikes. Now she was angry and caffeinated to boot.

"I know," I said gently. "But you did do it, Jac. You *did* do it. I know you don't like the way it happened. But aren't you at all, like, happy? Jac, you made a difference that no one else could. You *saved* them."

Jac picked up a cookie, examined both sides of it, and put it back on the plate. She picked up a brownie and began examining that.

"Whether or not I'm happy is *entirely* beside the point," Jac said. Her voice had softened more. Her examination of the brownie was apparently satisfactory, because she took a bite.

"Oh, no, it isn't," I said, slipping my arm through hers. "Jac, my God. You're, like, a genius! Hearing you play . . . I had no idea!"

"Like buttering me up is going to work," Jac muttered, looking very much to me like it *was* working.

Brooklyn Bigelow chose this moment to flounce by.

"Our act so left you in the *dust*, Cello Girl," Brooklyn called over her shoulder. "Sorry, loser."

Jac and I stared at each other, then simultaneously broke into wild giggles.

"Well! I guess she showed *you!*" I said.

"I'll never meet Simon Cowell now," Jac said mournfully, through a big grin.

"Jac," I said suddenly, taking her hand. "I'm sorry. Are you seriously really mad at me? I thought, I felt — I thought it was the right thing to do. Suzanne played. You played. Miss Wittencourt heard it all! I thought I was setting everything to right again. But I don't want to lose my best friend."

"Your only friend," Jac said, pursing her lips to hide a smile.

"My *only* friend. I don't want to lose my best and only friend."

Jac handed me a cookie.

"There might be a bug in that," she said. "I can't tell in this light."

I took a big bite.

"Crunchy," I said.

"Definitely a bug," Jac said. "Probably one of those Japanese beetles."

"Protein!"

In the center of the gym, Brooklyn had begun dancing to a popular song. She was copying something Beyoncé did in her latest video, and the move wasn't really translating. Above her head hung streamers and banners covered with cutout stars, moons, and gems. One of them fell off a streamer, floated down, and stuck to the top of Brooklyn's head. Unaware, she continued gyrating ineffectually.

"Now, that really pulls the outfit together," Jac remarked, and I giggled.

As if on cue, another shape fell off the dance banner and landed, tape side down, on Brooklyn's chest. She saw it and tried to swat it off without breaking her rhythm, of which she had very little.

Then in a flash it was happening everywhere. Stars, diamonds, even the streamers themselves were becoming unattached and drifting down, like an invisible force was directing them. A diamond stuck to Brooklyn's butt. A star and moon stuck, one on each knee. A streamer landed on her neck, and as Brooklyn tried to wave it away it curled around her like a scarf. A red moon became affixed to her ear, looking like a giant lipstick mark. Within seconds, Brooklyn was a veritable universe of cutout heavenly bodies. Every time she pulled one off, another seemed to sail down and attach itself to her. No one else seemed to be affected. No one tried to help her. For a second, her eyes met mine. I winked. From somewhere behind us, I heard an angry yell.

"Brook, what are you *doing?*"

Shoshanna Longbarrow barreled past us.

"Do you have any idea how long those took to cut out? I had to do them all *myself!!* They aren't for you to play with! You're ruining everything!!"

Brooklyn was trying to shriek some kind of explanation, but it came out sounding like the call of a whooping crane I'd seen recently on an Animal Planet documentary. Shoshanna took Brooklyn firmly by one star-bedecked arm and dragged her out of the gym.

"What in the world was that?" Jac said between guffaws.

"I think," I said, taking another small bite of Jac's buggy cookie, "that Suzanne Bennis just gave us a parting gift."

Chapter 17

Jac and I, by special dispensation courtesy of my mother, left the dance early and went out, just the two of us, to the local Chinese restaurant. As an appetizer, we had ordered a pupu platter, to our great amusement. The joke was no way shared by our waiter, who glowered whenever he looked at us.

"Pupu plattahhhh," Jac said, relishing every syllable. "Pupuuuuuuuu."

"Okay, enough, Maestra," I said severely. "I'm starving; we can't get kicked out of here."

"Yes, Voodoo Mama. Your words are my command."

I smirked and took a sip of my green tea.

"So we really helped Suzanne? And Miss Wittencourt?"

"We helped them," I replied. "You were the key, Jac. They're okay now."

"You're sure?"

"I'm positive, Jac. I was with Miss Wittencourt for a few moments before the cab came to take her home."

"And what did she say?"

"You know, she didn't say a thing, Jac. Not one thing. But her face...I know it sounds crazy, but just looking at her I could see something inside her had changed. A burden had been lifted. And just before she walked away, she gave me this nod. Just like, yeah. An affirmation."

"She didn't even say anything about

me?" Jac asked, ripping open three sugar packets simultaneously and pouring them into her tea.

"Jac, she had these tears in her eyes . . . and I knew they weren't just for Suzanne. They were for you, too. They were happy tears."

"Happy. That's going to be one interesting cello lesson I have tomorrow."

"I wish I could be there!" I said. Now that I had heard Jac play, I didn't think I could ever get enough of it. "Dollars to doughnuts she's going to give you that scholarship!"

"Bite your tongue, Voodoo Mama. You need to lie low for a while so I can figure out how to handle things," Jac said, giving me a huge grin. I grinned right back at her.

Our moment was interrupted by the appearance of our waiter carrying our pupu platter.

"Yum. *Yum!* So what do you mean, figure out how you're going to handle things?"

Jac sliced a scallion pancake into quarters with surgical precision, contemplating the first quarter very seriously before taking a bite.

"I mean just what I say. It's good to know I can play again, Kat. It is. But I'm realizing now that's only part of it. I have to decide if I *want* to play now. I might not want that scholarship."

"But . . . but . . ."

I poured more tea as a distraction. This was a complication that quite frankly had never occurred to me.

"I know, Kat. But you've got to understand something. I was born with this gift, okay? I accept that. But I never had this little introduction period, like you've had with your spirit sight. I never had the chance to

think about what it meant to be a professional performer, to study and practice and
basically give my life to my music. You've
gone through this whole process since I've
known you, where you went from admitting
to someone that you'd come into this sight —
big step, I know — to kind of grappling with
whether or not you wanted to let people know
that you're special in that way. To now. When
you seem to accept it — that you're a medium
and that it's part of you, and that, comfortable or not, it's going to be in your life. You
decided to use your gift, and to share it."

I nodded, feeling suddenly very grown-
up sipping my tea and watching Jac's ultra-
serious expression.

"But it wasn't like that for me, Kat. I can
do what I can do — I was born that way. But
nobody ever asked me what I *wanted*. And I
was too young to ask myself, or to know

I was entitled to an opinion about my own life. I was taking lessons on the cello by the time I was four years old. And because I was so good, it just became, like, this assumed thing . . . that this was my life. Because I was good, but even more because it was what my mother wanted."

Unlike my mom, who knew I'd come into the sight but waited for me to come to terms with it myself, in my own time, I thought.

"What exactly was it with your mother? She aspired to some kind of performing career and didn't make the cut?" I asked.

"Yes and no," Jac said. "Oh, my God, have you tried a dumpling? It's like a *poem!*"

I had actually just crammed an entire dumpling in my mouth at that moment, so I just nodded enthusiastically and pointed to my mouth.

"Yeah, right? So, anyway, with my mother, I guess her parents just didn't make her music a priority. It was more, like, something an educated girl just did, you know? Paint, or take ballet, or in her case play the viola. Playing professionally wasn't an option for her. Generation thing, you know. She was supposed to be a wife in training."

Not the area of that particular generation that my mother came from, I thought, though Jac's mother looked a good ten years older than mine. And then again, pretty much everything about my mother was different.

"So she just kind of made the decision for you, then," I said, having finally gotten most of the dumpling down.

"That's exactly what she did," Jac said. "And I think that had something to do with why I couldn't play after the Carnegie Hall thing. My body just took matters into its own hands — nice mixed metaphor, right? And *blam*. Suddenly, I just couldn't play. Now I can, but the bigger issue still isn't decided. You know, who I want to be. I don't want to just be handed some scholarship with the assumption that it's what I want. I have to be the one to decide."

Jac began cutting into a butterfly shrimp aggressively.

"You realize, Maestra, that at some point you're going to have to share these feelings with your mother? Whatever you decide, you have to talk to her about it."

Jac scowled, and cut harder. She suddenly detached half the shrimp with such force it flew off the plate and bounced gracefully against the fish tank before rolling under a table.

Jac looked momentarily embarrassed, then realizing no one but me had seen the flight of her warp-speed shrimp, she burst into a series of cackles. As usual, her laugh was contagious, and as we both let loose and howled, I noticed the waiter giving us a gloomy, suspicious look from his station.

Jac was right — she *was* my best and only friend. Such a strange mix. She played the cello like a tiny red-haired Yo-Yo Ma, dressed like a first lady, and read *Star* magazine religiously. And other than my mother, Jac was the most completely truthful person I'd ever met. Truthful about everything and to everyone but her mother. Which was kind of how I'd started out when I saw my first spook.

"I'm thinking we ought to have that fried banana thing for desert," Jac said.

I understood. I didn't want to talk about Jac's mother anymore, either.

"One fried banana *each*," I corrected. "Like my mom always says, in for a penny, in for a pound. Oh, my God, I completely forgot to tell you something!"

Jac looked up with a pleasant smile of anticipation.

"I got something for us, well, not exactly for us, but . . ." I groped in my purse. "I've had it in my bag all day but there was never a good time to show you."

"Produce it, Voodoo Mama; the suspense is killing me!" Jac said.

I pulled my hand out of the purse and held the thing out in front of Jac.

"A red bandanna?" Jac asked.

I nodded.

"For Max," I said. "I think you should hang on to it until the next time you come over, so you're the one to put it on him."

Jac took the bandanna with a smile so

wide you'd have thought I handed her an autographed picture of Orlando Bloom. Then she started to laugh, and that got *me* laughing. I have no idea what was funny. We were just happy.

At the next table, I noticed a thin, graying man smile in our direction. He was seated alone, reading a copy of the *New York Times* that had a front-page headline about President Lyndon Johnson. Apparently, this restaurant had been here a really long time. I smiled back at him, and he took a bite of something that had probably not been on the menu for a few decades. So many spirits wanted something. But a lot didn't — they just wanted to be seen. I could see them. I was happy to.

One moo goo gai pan with extra rice and one fried banana later, I stood outside waiting for my taxi. My mother had given us both cab fare home, and Jac had already been picked up. My taxi arrived shortly thereafter, and I climbed in and settled comfortably in the back seat. It was nice sometimes to be an anonymous passenger, to sit back and let someone else do the driving. To not have to talk about anything.

We drove past the school on the way home. The dance was long over, and the school was completely dark. The library windows reflected moonlight, looking like pairs of eyes in the blackness. I felt a shiver down my spine as I suddenly remembered that Suzanne Bennis had not been the only otherworldly presence in that library. That dark, empty shadow I'd seen. The one that buzzed with malevolence. Whatever it was, I knew one thing. It was still there. And what was worse, I knew that after my interaction with Suzanne, that thing now knew about *me.* I had gotten its attention. And it wasn't going to go away. Eventually I'd have to confide in Jac about what I'd seen. And my mother as well. We'd have to sort out what that thing was. We'd need a plan. But I didn't want to think about that now. Let it wait until the sun was safely high in the sky.

I was relieved when we turned down a side street and left the school alone back in the dark. I had a quick vision of Brooklyn Bigelow covered in dance decorations, and I almost laughed out loud. I thought about the unexpected civility of Shoshanna after I brought up her grandmother. Where had that come from?

Shoshanna *had* said she now felt much better about her grandmother since . . . something she stopped herself from saying. Was it possible Shoshanna had gone to my mother for help? Had my mother gotten a message across to her from her grand-mother?

My mother never talked about her clients' identities, and I certainly knew better than to ask. My suspicion that Shoshanna had sought my mother's help would remain just that — a suspicion. But it was more than that, too. In a way, it was hope. Hope that Shoshanna Longbarrow, the zip code's Most Popular Girl and Celestial Ruler of the Satellite Girls, might, just possibly, not be so closed-minded as I'd thought. Hope that not all popular, *normal* girls were like Brooklyn Bigelow. Hope that maybe when you got right down to it, no one person was necessarily what they seemed on the surface.

We pulled onto the street where I lived, and the taxi stopped outside my house. Most of the lights were out. The kitchen was illuminated by the gentle, golden hue of several beeswax candles. I heard Max begin to bark inside, and as always the sound filled my heart with love. And at the same time, I couldn't *wait* to see my mother.

I didn't know what lay in my future. Just that there would be a bunch of regular stuff, and a bunch of unusual, important stuff. That to the dead, I *was* the most popular girl in school. A translator, a messenger. Sometimes a savior. Sometimes simply a friend. And if I developed a passion for soy patties and harem pants and preferred to work by candlelight, and if I carried a deck of tarot cards with me when I traveled and developed a reputation for talking to myself, well, then, that was just how it was going to be.

So, yeah, it isn't necessarily the coolest thing in the world to be a medium.

But then again, it *could* be.